"Wait here,"
Luis gestured

As he strode off toward the helicopter, Cal perched on the edge of a huge block that formed a low table at the pyramid's base.

Cal watched Luis—those long legs—the easy animal-like grace of his walk. Then he was back, standing over her, lightly swinging a machete so that the sunlight bounced off its wicked blade.

"Maybe I should have mentioned a local superstition," he said. "Women come to sit on that stone to ensure they produce a large family."

As she leaped to her feet, she heard a soft chuckle. "I shouldn't worry, *querida*. After all, surely it has more to do with the lady's husband than a chunk of inanimate stone. Wouldn't you agree?"

RACHEL FORD was born in Coventry, descended from a long line of Warwickshire farmers. She met her husband at Birmingham University, and he is now a principal lecturer in a polytechnic school. Rachel and her husband both taught school in the West Indies for several years after their marriage and have had fabulous holidays in Mexico, as well as unusual experiences in Venezuela and Ecuador during revolutions and coups! Their two daughters were born in England. After stints as a teacher and information guide, Rachel took up writing, which she really enjoys doing the most—first children's and girls' stories, and finally romance novels.

Books by Rachel Ford

HARLEQUIN PRESENTS
1160—A SHADOWED LOVE
1304—LOVE'S FUGITIVE
1337—WEB OF DESIRE

HARLEQUIN ROMANCE
2913—CLOUDED PARADISE
3116—LOVE'S AWAKENING

RACHEL FORD

lord of the forest

Harlequin Books

TORONTO • NEW YORK • LONDON
AMSTERDAM • PARIS • SYDNEY • HAMBURG
STOCKHOLM • ATHENS • TOKYO • MILAN

Harlequin Presents first edition June 1991
ISBN 0-373-11368-4

Original hardcover edition published in 1990
by Mills & Boon Limited

LORD OF THE FOREST

PROLOGUE

'*SEÑOR! Un momento, señor.*'

The man was loading wooden packing-cases into the back of a Land Rover. He ignored the insistent call until— '*Por favor, señor.*' The speaker, a stout, khaki-clad airport official—well, virtually the only official at the small inland airstrip—was at his shoulder now like a buzzing gadfly, and with a barely concealed grimace of irritation the man set down the box he was holding and slowly turned.

'What is it?' His Spanish, unlike the other's softer, more feminine Latin-American pronunciation, had the hard classical Catalan accent.

'You are returning to Chicambo, *señor?*'

He picked up the final case and dumped it in the vehicle. 'Yes.' His tone was not encouraging, but the other persevered.

'There is a young man—a boy,' he amended. 'English.' He gestured towards the small duplex hut, sweltering almost visibly under a rusting red corrugated-iron roof, which served as departure and arrival lounge. 'He wishes to go to the village.'

'So?' The man was turning away, already reaching into his jeans pocket for his keys.

'But, *señor*, he was expecting to be met and no one has come for him. Perhaps you would——?'

'No.' The man did not raise his voice, but the

tone was a cold rebuff. 'I do not give rides to hippies, back-packers.'

'This one is—different, *señor*. He is too young to be alone here—still a puppy, wet behind the ears.' He shrugged, as if in apology for his tender-heartedness, and the other looked down at him thoughtfully.

'You know, I do believe, Basilio, that you are becoming sentimental in your old age.'

'Perhaps. But if you would only see him——' Then, as the man inserted the key into the lock, Basilio added, a shade desperately, 'It is fortunate that Lieutenant Ramirez is not here this afternoon. You know how he is with boys, and this one . . .'

He spread his hands in a graphic gesture, and, at the thought of Ramirez's pudgy face, a mask of gross, thick-lipped sensuality, the man's own lips twisted in distaste. He straightened up and gestured impatiently to Basilio to lead the way.

The air in the small room was dank and fetid, a swarm of flies droning dispiritedly in endless spirals around the ceiling. The sole occupant was sitting on the only bench. He was clad in baggy, camouflage-type drill trousers and combat jacket, a khaki drill hat jammed down over his fair hair, and his hands were thrust deep in his pockets, his long legs sprawled in front of him as he disconsolately surveyed the scuffed toes of his trainers.

For a moment, the man gazed down at him unseen. Basilio was right, damn him. Whether it was the fragile-looking wrists, the soft line of the chin—which was all that was visible of the face—the boy had a certain quality, a vulnerability, and just for a fleeting second a wholly unexpected feeling of compassion stirred within the man's frozen heart.

Then his companion was bending over the boy. '*Señor.*' And, startled, the lad was looking up, first at the speaker, but then past Basilio's broad shoulder, huge, dark-lashed gold-topaz eyes widening as they locked with his own . . .

CHAPTER ONE

A TRICKLE of sweat ran down between Cal's shoulder-blades and she shifted her position slightly on the hard bench, staring down at an enormous red ant that, having navigated her rucksack, was now advancing purposefully on her white trainers.

What am I doing here? she asked herself despairingly. What am I doing here? Help, somebody, please help. I feel awful. The flight down from Santa Clara in that horrible matchwood plane . . . that electric storm . . . I swear I saw lightning bounce off the wing beside me . . . and that landing-strip—like a switchback, ugh! And my arm. I wondered why the doctor asked me if I was right- or left-handed just before she shot the first jab in. Now, I shall never be able to use it again . . .

And where's Pete Sanderson got to? He's supposed to be meeting me, isn't he, to drive me out to Chicambo? I thought Americans were supposed to be well organised, certainly well enough organised to be able to meet their latest recruit, who's come all this way to do her bit for the rain forests of San Cristóbal. Oh, damn all tropical rain forests—and damn Phil! If it wasn't for him . . .

'*Señor.*'

I'm going to be sick. I know I am.

8

'*Señor!*'

Cal looked up reluctantly. Silhouetted against the brilliant sunlight in the doorway, a plump man in khaki trousers and sweat-stained shirt was bending towards her. *Señor*? He must think she was a man. She opened her mouth, but then closed it again. No need to put him right—in fact, maybe it was all to the good.

Just for once in her life, she was actually grateful for her tall, slender build, and the kind of looks that her friends called gamine and her non-friends tomboy; for the thick, short-cropped tawny-blonde hair and shaggy fringe; for the heart-shaped face, with the liberal sprinkle of freckles and the open, engaging grin, which showed a mouthful of strong white teeth.

Behind him, she saw now, was another, much taller man. He was staring down at her over the plump man's shoulder, frowning with the effort to focus on her after the dazzle outside. His own face was in deep shadow, so that she could make out nothing apart from the lean outline and the one lock of jet-black hair across his brow.

She sensed rather than saw the penetrating pair of eyes which were subjecting her to a cold, dispassionate scrutiny. The man had not spoken, had made no move towards her, his hands were thrust into his jeans pockets in an almost negligent gesture, and yet there was something about him, a potency—wholly unconscious, she was sure—which emanated from him even while he did not move a muscle.

She tore her eyes away and looked back at his

companion.

'*Sí?*' She deepened her already husky voice a few notches, trying to inject a masculine timbre which she hoped would mask the slight tremor.

'*Señor*, you wish to get to Chicambo.' Through her misery, she felt a slight lift. She could follow his guttural tones—so her one year of subsidiary Spanish had not been wasted, after all. 'This gentleman is going there, so——'

A telephone shrilled from the other side of the flimsy partition wall. He stopped short, and, waving a hand in apology, disappeared. A few seconds later the strident ringing stopped and they heard his voice raised in animated conversation.

Cal realised that she was fiddling with one of the buttons on her camouflage jacket. She moistened her dry lips and gave the other man a wary smile as she racked her tired brain for something—anything—to say. But the stranger abruptly broke the silence for her.

'If you're quite ready——'

In spite of the overt hostility in his tone, a gush of relief flowed through her. Not Spanish, not even English with a Spanish accent, but pure American. Of course! What a fool she was. He must be Pete Sanderson—late, not the slightest word of apology, but at least he'd got here now.

She scrambled to her feet, almost tumbling over her rucksack and travel bag. 'Thank goodness you're here.' She grinned at him and gave a gusty sigh of relief. 'I was beginning to think I was going to have to walk all the way.' Then, when he still made no move towards her, only stared down at her in that narrow-eyed scrutiny, 'I'm Cal Ward,' she said and put out her hand, but he ignored it.

Well, she thought, welcome to San Cristóbal, Cal. So glad you could make it. I hope the trip was OK. Oh, thank you, Pete, yes, it wasn't too bad, and I've been really looking forward to working with you. What was wrong with him, for heaven's sake? Americans were an open-hearted, matey bunch, weren't they? But she must be charitable. According to his doctorate thesis, which she'd skim-read on the dog-leg London-Miami-Santa Clara flight, he'd been out here for over three years, so perhaps after all that time surrounded by steaming rain forests the sweetest disposition was liable to turn sour. All the same, though, she was doing him a favour, wasn't she, coming out here, so he might at least make some—

'If you're quite ready,' he repeated impatiently, so that her hackles rose even more.

Still, she managed to keep her tone cool as she replied, 'Yes, certainly.'

He nodded brusquely and turned towards the door. She realised that, half unconsciously, she had been waiting for him to pick up—or at least offer to carry—her rucksack and bag. But clearly chivalry was way down on this man's list of priorities. Perhaps that was it. She knew that all his previous fieldworker assistants had been men; maybe he resented being saddled, as he saw it, with a woman, and was determined to show her right from the start that she could expect no favours. Well, she'd just have to show him, right from the start, that she was at least as good as any two men.

She jutted her jaw pugnaciously, bent down to take a firm grip on her luggage, and hurried after him.

But then the nausea which had been lurking in the undergrowth for hours suddenly took control, so that she dropped her bags and clapped her hand wildly to her mouth. He turned in the doorway.

'What's the matter now?'

Through her fingers she mumbled, 'I f-feel sick.'

'Oh, for——'

He placed a hard hand on her arm and rapidly propelled her towards a rickety door in the corner of the room. She stumbled in, dragging the door to behind her, and proceeded to throw up everything, right down to the bacon sandwiches and coffee she had unwisely had for an early breakfast at Heathrow.

When eventually she emerged, pale and slightly unsteady at the knees, there was no sign of him. She could have been dying in there, for all that unfeeling swine cared. Her luggage had disappeared though, and when she went in search of it she found that her reluctant host had dumped it in the back of an old Land Rover. Now he was leaning up against the vehicle, his arms folded, and from under the brim of an old straw hat he was scowling across the sizzling tarmac in her direction. Cal could feel that scowl at twenty paces, as though it were a hail of barely invisible bullets.

Oh, God, what was she going to do? How was she ever going to be able to work with him? She couldn't, she just couldn't. She was tired, dispirited, empty, sticky all over, and now, at the sight of him, she had to resist the almost overpowering urge to plump down on to the dusty ground, right where she was standing, and burst into a torrent of self-pitying tears. But if she did that he would almost certainly lose all patience with her, hurl her luggage back on to the tarmac and drive off without her.

She braced her jelly-like knees and, tilting her head at a defiant angle, walked across to him. As she approached he straightened up and, without a word, threw open the passenger door. Not looking at him, she climbed in.

'I beg your pardon?' His tone was polite uninterest.

'I said, yes, thank you, I feel much better.'

She congratulated herself on—almost—keeping the snap out of her voice. The next three months were clearly going to be a trying enough time for both of them without their coming to blows before they'd even left the airport.

She settled back into the seat and he got in beside her, reaching across to pull her door to. His arm brushed against her thigh so that under the crumpled cotton of her trousers she felt the tiny hairs stir and stand erect. Surreptitiously, she edged away, her leg still uncomfortably prickling from the casual touch of his fingers, and pressed herself against the door.

The man at the gate gave what was surely an exaggeratedly obsequious salute for a dirty old Land Rover, then threw open the barrier with an expansive gesture and they swung out on to a wide, unmetalled road which led through the outskirts of the town.

It was, presumably, one of the poorer areas, and as they threaded their way through the bicycles and mule carts, the beat-up Cadillacs and garishly painted trucks and buses, all of them driven kamikaze-style by drivers as apparently intent on their own destruction as on that of anyone who happened to stray into their path, Cal caught glimpses of narrow alleys leading between single-storeyed, one-roomed shacks. But despite the squalor, and her companion's continuing morose silence, she all at once became tinglingly aware of the excitement mounting within her. She was here, she really was *here*! In less than a day, she was half a world away from the drabness of London, away from the grey misery that had engulfed her ever since the dreadful humiliation of just eight days ago.

Unable to keep away any longer, she'd returned a day early from the anti-nuclear-power-station demo and gone to her fiancé Phil's flat, only to discover him in bed with a woman they'd met casually at a party a few nights before. She'd crept away unnoticed, like a stricken animal . . .

And yet, was she really in San Cristóbal? On either side of the street huge hoardings clamoured the delights of Coke, Pepsi, Seven-Up and Kentucky Frieds.

'I suppose if you're ever feeling homesick you just take a drive along here,' she said brightly.

'What?' He glanced briefly at her.

'You know—all these.'

She gestured towards the billboards and smiled

invitingly, but he merely raised one quizzical eyebrow and relapsed into his taciturn silence.

OK, you be like that, she thought angrily. I know it was a pretty feeble effort, but can't you even share a joke?

They were soon clear of the town and the road led as straight as any Roman highway through the flat landscape, fields of what she presumed was sugar-cane flowing away from them on either side. There was far less traffic now, although every so often they had to swing out to avoid wandering groups of scrawny-looking cattle and goats. One animal had clearly not been so lucky, for ahead of them Cal saw a gaggle of scavenging turkey vultures. As they sped past the birds rose reluctantly in a black, flapping cloud to reveal the bloody, half-dismembered corpse.

Her stomach began to heave again and she looked hastily away, only to glimpse what she was certain was a flicker of sardonic amusement cross her companion's lips. Her mouth tightened, but even as she went to turn away she found her unwilling gaze held as though by some magnetic force. For the first time she really looked at him, and she felt her jaw sag with disbelief. How astonishingly handsome he was—never, in all her life, had she seen such a face.

She studied him surreptitiously at first from under the brim of her drill hat, then, as all his attention remained seemingly on the road ahead, with increasing boldness.

His face was square cut, the firm lines of his deeply tanned features emphasised by the black

hair, which was slightly curling into the neck . . .
the nose well-shaped, aquiline, though in profile
almost hawklike . . . thin but sensual mouth . . .
thick, sooty eyelashes beneath fine, dark brows . . .
A thoroughly handsome—no, handsome was a
wholly inadequate word for such a—beautiful face.

And yet . . . Despite the burning heat, she
shivered slightly. Somehow, she sensed that this
beauty was of a wholly aloof, forbidding kind.
There was a hard, intimidating quality to that
face—as though, she thought suddenly, he'd
brought down an invisible shutter between himself
and the rest of the world, or, at any rate, between
himself and her.

And, on second thoughts, maybe that was just
as well. In her desperate need to get away from
London, from her office—and most of all from
Phil's vicious phone calls when, after a sleepless
night, she'd sent back his ring—she'd impetuously
applied for the job advertised in the supporters'
newsletter which she herself edited in her role as
Information Officer for the conservation pressure
group Planet Earth Tomorrow. 'Wanted! ! !
Fieldworker to join Dr Pete Sanderson and his
small team in Chicambo, San Cristóbal,
undertaking ecological survey of Central
American rain forest. Three months' contract. Low
pay, long, exhausting hours, but a chance in a
million to do something really worthwhile for this
endangered environment.'

But in the few frantic days following her abrupt
decision she had by no means sorted out her
emotional turmoil, and an invisible shutter

between herself and any man was welcome.

They must have been driving for well over an hour, and Cal was just beginning to ask herself how much longer their silent ride would last when her companion lifted one casual finger from the steering-wheel.

'Chicambo's up there.'

She leaned forward eagerly in her seat and strained her eyes into the heat haze. Far ahead of them she could just make out a line of low hills, tinged with a greenish smudge. That must be the beginnings of the rain forest—somewhere in there was to be her home for the next three months.

They had left the lowland plain now and were climbing steadily. Instead of the cane plantations, the road was bordered by scrub which at intervals had been cleared around small clusters of wooden, thatch-roofed huts. As they raced past, Cal glimpsed groups of women bending low over rows of long-leaved shrubby plants . . . a man slicing a huge hank of green bananas from a palm-fronded tree . . . two young black-haired children—a boy and a girl, neither of them more than four years old—holding out to them something grey and lizard-like and wriggling, hanging helplessly upside down from string tied round its tail.

'What's that?'

'Iguana. They were hoping you'd buy it.'

'Buy it? What, to keep?'

He laughed scornfully. 'No, to eat, of course. They're quite delicious, roasted.'

Aghast, she stared at him, her eyes open wide.

'You mean to say you've actually eaten them?'

'On occasion, yes.'

'But that's terrible.' Her voice was shaking.

'Really?' he replied coldly. 'Any worse than you indulging in such European delicacies as frogs' legs?'

She swelled with indignation. 'I can assure you that I have *never* in the whole of my life eaten frogs' legs—and I have no intention of eating iguana, either.'

He lifted one shoulder in a lazily insolent shrug. 'Suit yourself. And maybe you'd like me to turn round so that you can deliver a sermon to those people back there on how to organise their economy so that it doesn't offend your moral susceptibilities.'

She flushed angrily under the stinging sarcasm. 'No, thank you. You'll be surprised to learn that I've got slightly more sensitivity than to dream of lecturing the people I'm going to be working among for the next three months.'

'Working?' The surprise broke through his deliberately even tones. 'You mean to say you're here to work?'

'Well, of course I am.' Was he being stupid or was she? 'I'm your new PET.'

'My what?' For the first time in their brief acquaintance she actually seemed to have penetrated his chill composure, and he flashed her a very peculiar, almost alarmed look.

'You know—Planet Earth Tomorrow.'

'You're from Planet Earth Tomorrow?' he said slowly.

'That's right.' She grinned happily at him and prodded the small blue and red metal badge on her left lapel. Then all at once, as the full import of his words struck her, her smile faded.

'You—you did get the telex about me, didn't you? Jake—my boss—sent it via the PET group in Santa Clara.' When he did not reply, she went on flatly. 'You weren't expecting me, were you? You just happened to be at the airport.' Dismay and horrified embarrassment were welling up inside her. 'You must have wondered who the heck I was. I'm so sorry—it was all such short notice.'

He remained silent, but, despite her embarrassment, relief was now slowly oozing through her. That was the reason for his unfriendliness, his downright hostility. 'You probably thought I was some sort of scrounging freeloader or—or something. No wonder you weren't very—I mean . . .'

She floundered to a halt. The shock—coupled with the heat and a horribly empty stomach—was making her light-headed, and she heard herself babbling on uncontrollably, 'You know, it only goes to show just how deceptive first impressions can be.'

'Really?' He was all polite interest.

'Yes, if I'd met you in other circumstances, I'd have put you down as—oh, a Spanish, or at least a San Cristóbal grandee.' She wrinkled her snub nose. 'You know the type.'

'Enlighten me.'

His lack of response disconcerted her again, but she pressed on. 'Well, the sort who lives in some fabulous hacienda like——' she jabbed with her finger to where, on a hillside surrounded by lush greenery, she had just caught a momentary glimpse of a low, elegant white villa '—like that one over there. Pampered by dozens of servants, grinding his peasants into the dust and surrounded by five million hectares of land which he doesn't need.'

'Tell me.' His tone was contained, but somehow she sensed that beneath the evenness there was a barely suppressed anger. 'How long have you been in San Cristóbal?'

'Just since this morning, of course.'

'And how many previous visits have you made to this country?'

'None, but——'

'And how many other overseas trips have you made?'

'Well,' she was beginning to flounder under this relentless cross-examination, 'I did several field trips abroad when I was a student, and after I got my ecology degree I spent two months in Turkey studying the loggerhead turtle——'

'And I suppose you consider that this vast experience of yours gives you the automatic right to start setting to rights the political organisation of your host country?'

'No, of course not.' A self-defensive anger was stirring in her now. 'But if I haven't been here long enough, maybe you've been here too long. You've obviously been mixing with the wrong sorts. You—you've been got at, corrupted——'

She broke off abruptly and pressed her fingers

to her forehead, trying to put in order her tattered thoughts. There was something wrong here, terribly wrong. Everything she'd read and heard of Pete Sanderson had told her that he was a two hundred per cent dedicated, not to say fanatical scientist, who would never have allowed himself to be side-tracked into local politics. But in that case . . .

She swung round to face the man beside her and said abruptly, 'Who are you?'

Before he could reply, though, they had rounded a sharp left-hand bend and were confronted by a Jeep, skewed at a horrible angle into the deep ditch which ran beside the road. A still figure lay slumped, head lolled forward, in the driving seat.

Even as Cal gave a sharp exclamation of shock her companion had braked violently and was leaping from the vehicle down into the ditch. She followed, more slowly, terrified of what she would see, and by the time she had scrambled down the steep bank the casualty was being manoeuvred gently but firmly, in spite of his mumbled, incoherent protests, out of the cab.

'Sh-should you move him?'

'You want to leave him here?'

'But shouldn't we send for an ambulance?'

He shot her a derisive look. 'This isn't your precious England, you know. It'll take at least an hour to get an ambulance to him. For God's sake, come and help.'

Desperately trying to still her trembling hands, Cal moved forward, took hold of the man's legs and helped ease him free of the buckled cab.

Together, they propped him against the trunk of a small tree that was growing from the bottom of the ditch, and she forced herself to look at him.

He was thin, fair-haired, with an unkempt beard. His face was deathly white, apart from where bright red blood was oozing from a scalp wound, darkening the blond hair and dripping down his neck on to his white shirt. She swallowed hard against her protesting stomach as she saw that more blood was pumping from a deep gash in his forearm.

The other man was running his hands rapidly over the inert body and, without turning, he said curtly, 'First-aid box, under my seat.'

Only when she did not move did he swing round on her. 'Get it, will you?' he snarled. 'What the hell's the matter with you?'

She ran her tongue round her chalky lips. 'Is—is he dying?'

The contempt was unmistakable. 'He will be, if you don't pull yourself together. Call yourself a man?'

No, I don't actually, she wanted to shriek at him, but this was neither the time nor the place to put right this arrogant, overbearing stranger. Instead, she clawed her way up the steep bank and with shaking hands seized the metal box. Just for a moment she stood clutching it, trying to summon her last reserves of strength and courage, then, hearing him swear savagely, slid back down to him.

He had raised the man's arm and his fingers were clamped tightly over the wound.

'Bandage! Dressing!'

Fumbling among the unfamiliar labels, she found two soft packages marked '*venda*' and '*algodón*' and tore them open. She sensed him glance at her face, then he said, a shade less harshly, 'I'll do it. Put your fingers here and press hard.'

Thrusting from her the last vestiges of revulsion, she obeyed. He ripped off a length of bandage, made a pad of cotton wool, then, pushing her fingers clear, rammed it against the wound and began bandaging it tightly into place. As he was strapping the man's arm up against his shoulder with another length of bandage, the man gave a groan and opened his eyes for a second.

'I—I—'

'Shh. It's all right. You'll be OK.'

As Cal, hardly able to recognise the soothing voice, sat back on her heels, he picked up the man and carried him up the bank. She closed the lid of the box and hastily scrambled up after them, to see him already easing the man into the seat she had occupied. Without a word, she handed him the box and followed him round to the other side. He was climbing into the driver's seat when she at last found her voice.

'W-what about me?' She hoped she didn't sound too forlorn.

He looked down at her for a moment, his lips pursed, then swung himself down, went round to the rear of the vehicle, pulled out her rucksack and bag and dumped them unceremoniously on the dusty brown humps that passed for a roadside verge.

'Chicambo is a couple of kilometres ahead. You

can't miss it.' Then, as she stared at him, panic-stricken, he added with a flick of contempt, 'You're a fieldworker, aren't you? Well, try and behave like one—not like some fool of a tourist.'

'Oh, you——' He could perfectly well have made room for her in the back, among all those packing-cases, if he'd wanted to, and she would have happily gone into town and back again rather than be abandoned, but no—and no doubt he was enjoying her obvious discomfiture.

'Besides,' he added with a small, unpleasant smile, 'the walk'll do you good—get rid of some of that nasty temper of yours.'

He was leaning forward to switch on the ignition when she put a restraining hand on his bare arm. A horrible suspicion had been forming itself in her mind, and she had to know for sure.

'This man—do you know him?'

'Yes.' There was the faintest flicker of grim amusement. 'His name's Sanderson—Pete Sanderson.'

'So—who are you?'

'For what it matters to you—my name's Luis Revilla.'

She had to ask one further question, although she was already dreadfully certain of the answer. 'You live near here?'

'That's right. Back there—in that hacienda you so kindly pointed out to me.'

And then he had snatched the Land Rover into gear and was roaring off back the way they had come.

CHAPTER TWO

CAL stood watching until the cloud of reddish dust which was the Land Rover had disappeared into the hazy horizon. Beside her, nose-first in the ditch, was the other vehicle, totally useless, and that was all, apart from the ribbon of road and, on either side, green rolling waves of cacao trees, whose leaves rustled eerily as a hot breeze brushed them.

If this were a Hitchcock movie and I were Cary Grant, she thought involuntarily, this is precisely the point at which that sinister crop-spraying plane should make an appearance—and start spraying me. But there was no plane—nothing— so, after a few moments, she hoisted her rucksack up on to her back, wincing as, despite her care, the strap scraped across her throbbing left arm. Picking up her bag, she trudged off, every footstep sending up a mini cloud of gritty dust . . .

The village, when she eventually spotted it ahead—surely far more than two kilometres away?—was shimmering, mirage-like, in the afternoon heat. Perhaps it *was* a mirage—after all the events of today nothing would surprise her, she thought gloomily. But the first houses—wooden and thatched, like the others they had passed—turned out to be solid enough, and so did the fierce-looking mongrel dogs which bounded out, barking, as she approached, only to retreat to the shade again to continue scratching themselves.

She sensed eyes on her everywhere, though the black, shadowed doorways of the houses were empty, apart from a few barefoot children, but when she smiled and called a tentative '*Buenos días*', they instantly vanished. Cal's heart sank way down to her trainers. She had finally arrived, but, with Pete Sanderson at this very moment slumped unconscious in the front seat of that loathsome Land Rover, she had not the faintest idea where to go.

The street led into a small square, flanked on one side by the church—a stone-built, white-washed building topped by a small bell-tower, and the only structure of any substance in the entire place. She was just wondering whether to go in-side—there might be someone there she could ask directions from—when a middle-aged man, with a shock of white hair and clad in blue cotton shirt and trousers, appeared in the doorway.

He hurried down the steps towards her. 'And who might you be?' The Irish lilt was unmistakable.

'I'm Cal Ward. I—I've come to help Pete Sanderson with——'

'Yes, of course. He's expecting you. But, my poor girl,' his shrewd blue eyes seemed to take in everything of her at a glance, 'have you got here all on your own?'

The sympathy, balm though it was, was almost too much, and Cal just nodded.

'And what does that fellow Pete think he's doing, leaving you to find your own way here, then, in all this heat?'

'No, it wasn't like that——' Cal began, but he was already taking her bag from her and leading the way round the back of the church, where there was a small wooden bungalow with a deliciously shady veranda running the length of its front.

'Now you just sit yourself down there.' He gestured to a rickety-looking bamboo chair and regarded her closely. 'You look all in. What you need is a cold drink—or,' his blue eyes twinkled, 'would you prefer a cup of genuine English tea?'

Would she? 'Oh, I'd love one—thank you.' She smiled up at him, her dejected spirits beginning to creep back up again by the second.

'Right you are then. Iñéz.'

A stout, elderly woman—pure Indian, though she wore a European-style white dress and her thick, greying hair was arranged in an impeccable bun—appeared in the doorway. The man said something in a totally incomprehensible language, the woman nodded politely in Cal's direction, then withdrew as silently as she had come.

He settled himself in an even more battered chair. 'Now, let's introduce ourselves. I'm Father Aidan. I'm responsible for these people,' he nodded in the general direction of the village, 'and a dozen other villages, for my sins,' He extended a hard, callused hand and Cal took it. 'Now, tell me, what's that good-for-nothing Pete been up to?'

'I'm afraid he's had an accident, back there on the road. He's on his way to hospital now,' she went on hastily, as the priest, with an exclamation, leapt to his feet, 'and I'm sure he'll be all right.' I

certainly hope so, she added silently, but there was
no point in adding to her host's obvious distress.
'You see, we found him——'

'We?'

'Yes, it's all a bit complicated. You see, I was
waiting at the airport, when . . .'

The woman returned with a metal tea-tray and
Father Aidan poured two cups, strong and
fragrant, while Cal watched, almost whimpering
with pleasure.

'One of my little luxuries.' He smiled at her. 'I've
been out here over twenty years, but I still can't
stand the local coffee—tans the insides to leather.'

He added milk and passed her a cup. 'Now then,
so this man has taken Pete back to town. And did
this Good Samaritan happen to tell you his name?'

'Yes.' She hesitated, then, 'Luis Revilla. Do you
know him?'

'Of course. He lives——'

'Yes, I know. He told me.' Cal flushed as she
recalled the man's parting jibe and she felt the
priest's disconcertingly penetrating eyes linger on
her burning face for a moment.

'He knew Pete,' she added. 'He was able to tell
me who he was.'

'Oh, yes, he knows Pete well enough.' Father
Aidan's tone was dry.

'You mean, they don't get on?' Well, that was
hardly surprising. No one, surely, in their sane
mind would ever be able to get on with *him*. But
even so, she admitted grudgingly, that hadn't
stopped him doing everything he could to save
Pete's life back there.

'Well, let's just say they've had one or two differences of opinion—but there's no need for you to go bothering your head about that.'

Maybe not—certainly not just now, when she could feel the exhaustion creeping over her again—but there was something, definitely something. Was it just a personality clash—or was it to do with Pete's work? Certainly, Revilla's attitude towards her had seemed to become even more hostile when she'd told him she was from PET. In which case—her stomach contracted momentarily—with Pete at least temporarily out of action, she herself would be in the direct line of fire.

'And now, Cal—' the priest was getting to his feet '—you don't mind if I call you that, as you're going to be with us for some time?' She shook her head, smiling, and he went on, 'I'm due in one of my other villages, so I'll just take you to your quarters. I know Pete's been fixing up some sort of accommodation for you, although don't expect too many home comforts, will you?'

Cal dumped her rucksack on the narrow bed and surveyed what was to be her 'home' for the next three months. It was a funny feeling, alone in Pete's house—almost like turning up for a happily-anticipated party, and discovering that your host wasn't there. The house was a low, one-storeyed building with rooms opening off a long passage—kitchen, bathroom, living-room-cum-office, with a large desk piled with books and papers, a microscope and a portable typewriter, and Pete's bedroom, sparsely furnished, but with rows of bulging, neatly labelled plastic bags hanging from the open rafters.

Father Aidan had given her a quick tour of inspection and then roared off on a dilapidated though powerful motorbike, his cassock and communion bag stashed in a basket on the pillion seat.

Her room was large and had been whitewashed so recently that when she put her hand against the wall beside the bed it still felt damp. There was a large wooden cupboard, each of its four legs standing in small bowls of water, presumably to protect it from the ravages of termites, a bamboo table and chair, a white mosquito net draped behind the bed, and that was all.

Someone had closed the shutters against the heat. When she opened them, she saw that separated from the house only by a patch of rough ground and a wide, sluggish stream was the forest, green and mysterious—and beckoning. Tomorrow, Cal promised herself, tomorrow . . .

But in the meantime she was beginning to feel alarmingly light-headed once more—lack of food, she told herself reassuringly. Pete's dry goods store was filled to overflowing, and so was the bottled-gas refrigerator. Well, she certainly wasn't going to starve, she thought ironically—dedicated scientist he might be, but he obviously didn't neglect the inner man. But for tonight she eschewed the tinned ranks of ham, red salmon, chicken in tarragon jelly, and anchovy relish, and settled for easy-cook rice and chilli con carne, followed by a couple of the unfamiliar fruits which were in the refrigerator—apple-red, but with creamy flesh like a sweet pear.

While she ate, she contemplated her day—and what a day it had been. How ill Pete had looked . . . How long would he be away? Would she be able to manage on her own? Then, even less palatably, her encounter with Luis Revilla. What an abrasive, thoroughly unpleasant character he was . . . Still, it was a pity her tongue had, as usual, galloped away with her, given him that chance to snipe back at her about the hacienda. Although why should she care? And at least he hadn't realised she was a girl. 'Call yourself a man?' Momentarily, her lips twitched in wry amusement—that, in a way, was one minor triumph, and if she kept her head down, well, there was no need for their paths to cross again. He, no doubt, would be more than happy for her to keep her distance . . .

She yawned extravagantly. How tired she felt, but it was too early for bed. Maybe a shower would freshen her up, then she could spend a couple of hours looking through Pete's notes.

Her whole body was gritty with sweat. She eased her trainers away from her swollen feet with a groan of relief, then peeled off her clothes. In the tiny bathroom, a portable shower had been rigged up; she stood under the shower-head and gingerly pulled the handle. She gave a yelp as the jet struck her overheated face and body, but then relaxed into voluptuous enjoyment, letting the water course over her like cool silk. She could have happily stood under it for an hour, but the tank emptied with a gurgle and the water became a trickle.

Her skin was drying almost before she stepped out of the shower, but she wrapped herself in a towel, then, mopping her face with one corner, went out into the passage. Immediately, she collided with something solid and hard—and alive.

With a gasp of sheer terror she reeled back, then a pair of strong hands grasped her by the elbows. Her eyes were still full of water and the passage was almost dark now, but she recognised only too well the obstacle into which she'd just blundered.

'What the hell are you doing here?'

Her voice was an outraged squeak, then, as she felt the flimsy towel slip, she clutched at it, scowling fiercely up at him. But the scowl was wasted. She saw, with a *frisson* of alarm, that he was staring down, past her face, a faint crease of puzzlement between his brows. The alarm turned to panic and she went to move back out of reach, but too late. With the speed of a striking rattlesnake, his hand came up and the towel was wrenched brutally from between her frantically clawing fingers.

She just heard him give a sibilant hiss of astonishment, then, terrified, she leapt for her bedroom, but again he was too quick. He seized hold of her and spun her back round, holding her at arm's length, his fingers a steel trap on her delicate wrist.

'Well, well,' he said slowly. 'So, under those

appalling clothes, all *this* was hidden. No——'
warningly, as she struggled in his grasp. 'What was
it you said? Oh, yes, "It only goes to show just how
deceptive first impressions can be."'

'L-let me go, damn you!' she snarled, but his grip
only tightened bruisingly on her until she had to
bite her lip on a cry of pain. Then, with deliberate
slowness, he allowed his eyes the freedom of her
body, to travel in a lingering scrutiny over every
centimetre—her slim shoulders, her small, high
breasts, then down over the long curve of her
slender waist and hips, while she could only
glower helplessly at him from under her
tawny-blonde fringe, just grateful that in the
darkness of the passage he could surely not be
aware of the scorching burst of heat which was
spreading uncomfortably all over her skin,
tracking the course of his eyes.

Alongside the anger, fear was flaring wildly
inside her, but she thrust it down. 'Will you let me
go?' she said between her teeth. 'How dare you
come sauntering in here, without so much as a by
your leave? Get out, now, or I'll——'

'Or you'll what?' There was a glint of white teeth.
'Shout for help? Call the police? They'll have a
long journey from town, and in the meantime I
could be doing—well, *anything*.'

His voice dropped on the last word to a
menacing purr, and then, before she could do
more than tense, he bent down her wrist, jerking
her closer to him. Putting his other arm round her,
he drew her to him, pressing her into the strength
of his lean, hard body.

Then, even as she opened her mouth to protest, yell, even plead to be released, his mouth came down on hers and everything beyond the inexorable pressure of his lips, the musky smell of his warm skin, the hardness, the yielding softness of their bodies moulded together, was suddenly blotted out.

When he finally released her, he stared down at her, his breath warm against her cheek. Her blood was singing in her ears, she felt dizzy with—with what? A feeling, a wholly new feeling, that she could not identify, but which she knew instinctively was fraught with danger. Somehow, she dragged herself free of that unnerving sensation and, almost too shaken to speak, took refuge in anger. She put her hand to her mouth and fiercely wiped it across her lips.

'How dare you?'

He frowned at her gesture, but then shrugged. 'Put it down to an instinctive male reaction.' There was not the faintest whisper of apology in his voice. 'And besides—you fooled me once. I wanted to be certain this time that you are—what you seem to be.'

'Well, I hope you're satisfied now!' she snapped, and could have bitten her tongue off before the hasty words were half out of her mouth.

'Satisfied?' That throaty animal purr again. 'Oh, no, not in the least. In fact, you could say that my appetite has just been whetted.'

And before she could wrench herself free he had pounced, swift and lethal as a jaguar, and once again his mouth had clasped hers, ruthlessly smothering her furious protestations. His tongue, sweet as honey, forced her lips apart and began to gently probe her mouth, but she willed herself not to respond—she *would* not.

But then she felt his hands sliding over the silky skin of her spine, to rest across the small of her back, the pressure of his splayed fingers relentlessly forcing her body to meet his taut thighs, so that she could feel his tensed muscles through the thin cotton of his jeans. In spite of all her efforts, a long, slow shudder ran through her whole body and, her will-power crumbling to dust, she put her arms around him. With a little sigh, she yielded her mouth to his, as reality, space, time—all ceased to exist.

He was still holding her to him with one hand, but as the other began to caress her back again his arm brushed against hers. The touch was light enough, but red-hot jags of pain shot through her and she flinched away from him.

'What's the matter?' He was not quite in control of his voice.

Beads of sweat were breaking out on her forehead and she muttered between clenched teeth, 'My arm.'

His eyes took in her scarlet, swollen upper arm, then, without a word, he loosed her and stooped to pick up the towel which lay at her feet. He thrust it at her.

'Go and get some clothes on.'

There was a harsh edge to his voice now, and she stumbled into her bedroom, banging the door and leaning up against it, her arms outstretched

for support as she took in huge, painful gulps of
air until her lungs protested. She closed her eyes
and tried to still the violent trembling of her body,
still tingling from the touch of his hands. She
cringed inwardly. What unutterable folly had
possessed her to respond to his hateful advances
like—like some little tramp? Yes, she told herself
savagely, that was exactly how she'd behaved.
What lunacy! Half a day in San Cristóbal, that
was all it had taken for her to be suffering from a
severe case of tropical softening of the brain.

She knew instinctively that out there in the
passage he had been doing no more than amuse
himself, but that had been enough for her to
glimpse the lethal, sexual power of this man. If she
had half a grain of intelligence she would make
very certain that, here in Chicambo, miles from
anywhere, alone and unprotected, she never
allowed herself to get into a situation like that
again . . .

But what would she do if he ever chose to
unleash on her the whole weight of his physical
magnetism? Tell him to get lost, she told herself
fiercely. If need be, he would have to be taught
that, in her case at least, tropical brain fever was a
very short-lived phenomenon.

Nevertheless, she stayed in the bedroom for as
long as she dared, in fact until she was quite sure
that if she didn't make an appearance within the
next two minutes he would come in and fetch her.
Unable to stand even the touch of a blouse or
T-shirt against her throbbing arm, she knotted
herself very securely into her long, totally

unrevealing pink cotton wrap, and went through to the kitchen.

CHAPTER THREE

THE swift tropical dusk had fallen now and Revilla was just lighting the second of the large kerosene lamps which hung down from the ceiling. He glanced up as she came in, his face expressionless.

'Can you work these things?'

'Well, I've never tried.' She did her best to match his cool, offhand tone. 'But I've used hurricane lamps at home, so I should be able to.'

'Come here and I'll show you.' But she stood with the kitchen table between them as he went on, 'Just check that the wick is level before you light it, and be very careful how you put the chimney back on—so——'

He leaned forward, the glass cradled in his long, tanned fingers, frowning in concentration. The flicker of the flame shone directly up on to his face, illuminating it with a soft glow so that the harsh lines melted, the mouth had an illusory tenderness and the eyes, veiled by those sweeping black lashes——

As though sensing her attention on him rather than the lamp, he glanced up, and just for a second he held her gaze. Looking straight into his eyes, she realised for the first time just how dark and unfathomable they were; brown, yes, but the intense brown of bitter chocolate, almost black under the shadow cast by the lamp, except where she herself, a tiny gold pin-point, was reflected in each of the pupils.

All at once the room seemed to fill with a clamorous noise, then she had jerked back her head, as though the lamp's flame had burned her, and he was saying, 'Then you adjust the wick and haul it up—like this. Think you can manage that?'

'Oh, yes.' The tartness in her voice was only partly caused by his patronising tone. 'I'm not a totally helpless female, you know.'

He regarded her unsmilingly across the table. 'Now, your arm. Let me see it.'

'Oh, no—it's fine now, honestly.'

She shrank back from his outstretched hand, but found herself backing up between the fridge and the wall until there was nowhere else for her to go, and when he took hold of her arm to begin rolling up the loose sleeve of her wrap she could only stand unresistingly. This time, his touch was even more gentle, and when he softly butterfly-brushed across the taut, inflamed skin she flinched away once more from his cool fingertips, not through any pain, but because they were sending tiny, unnerving pinpricks of sensation, not just through her arm, but down through her shoulders, her breasts, and far, far deeper into her.

Dimly, she heard him give a sharp exclamation, then, 'What the hell have you done to yourself, for God's sake?'

'It—it's my injections,' she said huskily. 'I had to have them before——'

He took hold of her elbows, hooked one of the chairs out from the table with his foot, and sat her down in it. 'Don't move.'

In seconds, it seemed, he was back, carrying two bottles. He filled a glass with water, then held her palm and tipped two white tables into it. 'Pain-killers. Get them down you.'

As she forced herself to swallow, grimacing against the bitter taste, she heard him running more water, then he set down beside her a small bowl and poured in liquid disinfectant, turning the water into a white swirl.

'I couldn't see where Sanderson keeps his cotton wool, so . . .' From his jeans pocket he dug out a white handkerchief, still folded. He shook it out, dipped a corner of it into the liquid, then stroked it—icy cold—against the burning soreness of her flesh. Instantly, the throbbing pain began to ease. 'Yell out if I hurt you.'

Their eyes met again, then she nodded and looked away, resolutely keeping her gaze fixed on a knot in the table until he had finished. He soaked the handkerchief, folded it into a rough bandage, then wrapped it around her arm and knotted it.

'That should keep the bedclothes away from it.'

As she mumbled her thanks, he picked up the bowl and emptied it.

'How long ago is it that you had these jabs?'

'Oh, several days,' she said evasively.

'Hmm.' His gaze was unnerving. 'They must have filled you up with every goddamned thing they could lay their hands on, then bundled you straight up the plane steps. Is that how Planet Earth Tomorrow always works?'

There was a sneering note in his voice which

she did not like and she leapt to PET's defence. 'Oh, no—I needn't have come until the end of the month.'

'You were in a hell of a hurry to get out here then.' That coldly assessing scrutiny again.

'Oh, no. It was just, well, there were—reasons,' she added lamely. Such as I couldn't bear to risk setting eyes on my fiancé—sorry, my ex-fiancé— again, after I'd found him in bed with another woman. He'd already rung me several times, you see, after I'd sent back his ring—he'd been just wary at first, then angry, and finally crudely abusive. She closed her eyes on a grimace of pain, then opened them to find that intent gaze still on her.

'Arm still sore?'

She nodded. 'Yes, it is, rather.'

But she knew he didn't altogether believe her. He let it go, though, merely pulling out the chair opposite her to slide into it. Cal's heart sank. She had been fervently hoping that he would leave now, but he leaned back, his arms folded, as though he had every intention of staying the entire evening.

She opened her mouth to say, 'Look, do you mind? It's been a beast of a day,' but then she saw, for the first time, how pale and strained he looked. There were rusty brown stains across his blue T-shirt—Pete's blood. Of course, it had been quite a day for him, too—ever since he'd had his unwelcome passenger foisted on him at the airport. So instead she said, 'Would you like a drink? I saw some lager in the fridge.'

'If it's not too much hassle.' His tone was faintly

ironic; he had missed nothing of her inner struggle to be the welcoming hostess.

She stood up, moving awkwardly, conscious that his eyes were following her. She opened one can and poured the lager into a glass, smoking white with the cold, then she hesitated. She knew she shouldn't—not after those pain-killers—but her mouth and throat were achingly dry, so she opened a second one.

'Is that sensible?' His tone was such as he might use to a recalcitrant child.

'Yes, I think so,' she replied coldly, and held on firmly to her glass.

His lips tightened, but he only took a long pull at his drink, then said, 'Now, I seem to remember, before our little—er—digression, that you were asking me, in what no doubt is your usual gracious manner, what I'm doing here.'

Her hackles went up still further at his acid tone, but she contented herself with merely asking, 'Well?'

'I just thought you might be feeling some minute concern for your colleague. But I obviously overestimated you.'

She flushed under the rebuke—even though it was well deserved, she silently acknowledged, biting her lip in vexation. Since Revilla's arrival she had not given Pete's well-being a second's thought.

'Yes, of course I'm concerned,' she said in a low voice, studying the table. 'How is he?'

'Well, fairly comfortable now, and the doctors think he'll be OK—though he lost a lot of blood before we got to him.' Momentarily, her eyes strayed to those dark smears across the expanse of blue cotton. 'The arm should be all right, but he's also sustained a slight fracture of the skull.'

'Oh, no!' Cal was horrified. She sat silent, desperately sorry for Pete, but also——He was obviously going to be out of action for weeks, at least, and in that case . . .

'And so, Cal—it is Cal, isn't it?'

'Yes, Cal Ward,' she replied automatically.

'That's what I thought you said, back at the airport. But surely Cal—Calvin—is a man's name?'

She nodded. 'It can be, but my name's Calypso.'

'Ah, of course—Calypso.' He repeated the name, somehow making it sound like a beautiful, lilting melody. 'The nymph who entertained Odysseus, wasn't she?'

'Yes, that's right. I suppose you're thinking what a ridiculous name it is,' she said defensively, and pulled a face. 'Most people do—you know, quite unfitting for any sensible, down-to-earth twentieth-century woman.'

He drained his glass and set it down, then looked at her consideringly with his sombre brown eyes. 'No, I don't think it's in the least ridiculous. The name suits you perfectly.'

She was still trying to work out whether she had just been on the receiving end of a compliment or a subtle between-the-ribs insult, when he went on briskly, 'Now, to business. There will be no problem in arranging transport for you.'

Transport? She wrinkled her brow. Oh, of

course, he must be offering her a replacement vehicle until Pete's Jeep was back on the road. She really had misjudged him, she thought with a twinge of guilt, and smiled warmly across at him.

'Well, that's very kind of you. I——'

'The next flight for the UK is in two days, so if you'll let me know what time you want to leave——'

'Leave?' The word came out shrill and high. 'But I'm not leaving. I've only just got here, remember?'

'But you obviously won't be staying—not now.'

'Oh, and why not?' She tried, not altogether successfully, to keep the bristle out of her voice.

'Because you are a woman,' he said flatly and, seemingly quite oblivious to her gasp of outrage, made a sweeping gesture with his hands. 'This is no place for you, here on your own, without the comfort and security that a woman needs.'

She could hardly believe her ears. She'd heard, of course, of the notorious machismo streak of the Latin-American male, but this was her first experience of the phenomenon in full spate.

'You—you arrogant male pig!' she hurled at him, too angry to measure her words. 'If I'd had any idea of quitting—which I most certainly didn't have—of leaving with my tail between my legs, just because there isn't a big strong man——' she corrected herself '—macho man to look after me, I'm damned if I'll go now. Of all——'

'Be quiet.' A warning flush was spreading across his tanned cheekbones.

'No, I won't.'

Instinct told her that here was a man who was accustomed to instant obedience from all he met, but, whatever the usual gratifying result of a black-browed scowl, she certainly wasn't going to allow herself to be intimidated—even though, quite suddenly, she was beginning to feel very peculiar. She shook her head, to clear it of the odd sensation that someone was methodically filling it with straw.

'I've come out here to help catalogue all the plant species in the Chicambo reserve, and if I go now there'll be no one to carry on the work—at least, not straight away. And with Pete out of action as well, the whole project might fall apart——'

She broke off, her eyes narrowing in suspicion, as she recalled Father Aidan's veiled hints of conflict between Pete and this man, then she went on with sudden conviction, 'But, of course, that's precisely what you want, isn't it—us to go, and the project to be abandoned?'

He returned her gaze with matching hostility. 'Yes, I would be delighted.'

'But why?' Her anger was mingled now with bewilderment. 'Can't you see the value of what we're doing, battling to save what we can of the rain forests before they've all gone forever? Surely you don't want to see them all destroyed?'

'No, I don't. But I've no time for people like you, coming out here to my country for a few months with your half-baked ideas for saving us from our own ignorance—' his savage tone shocked her '—and then, having salved your ecological consciences, you can go safely back to your pampered existences.'

Cal stared at him, momentarily nonplussed. He

really did believe in what he was saying—seemed to feel the rightness of what he was saying at least as deeply as she. She wanted to reason with him, say, 'Look, you just don't understand.' But then she remembered the cardinal rule of the PET handbook still stowed away in her rucksack: 'Always respect the views of the local inhabitants,' which in this case could be roughly translated as: 'Don't tangle with the grandee from the hacienda on the hill', so she only muttered, 'That's just not fair.'

'Isn't it?'

'No, it's not. If people like me didn't care enough to do something for the environment——' She broke off, chewing her lip in frustration. 'But, whatever you think of the likes of me, aren't you forgetting Pete?'

'No,' he said grimly, 'I'm not forgetting him.'

'Well, then,' she burst out passionately, 'you can't lump him in with the rest of us. He's been working in San Cristóbal for years; he's making this place his life's work.'

'To achieve what precisely?'

The tightly spoken words were a douche of icy water in her face, but she swept on, 'He's the one who had the idea to buy this segment of forest from one of the local landowners—and it was PET that helped to raise the funds to do it,' she added defiantly. 'But, as well as studying it scientifically, he wants to make it a model, a microcosm of how the rain forests—not just here, but all over the world—can be preserved.'

He drew back slightly, as though he found her

enthusiasm distasteful, and his lip curled into a sneer. 'Yes, your Sanderson is quite a dreamer.'

'And what's wrong with that? If more people were dreamers and fewer were like——' A sudden urgent, warning voice in her ear made her break off abruptly. 'He's got the vision to see into the long term——'

'Dreamers, visionaries—they're all fanatics. And fanatics are—dangerous——' He broke off for a moment, seemingly lost in his own sombre thoughts, then went on, 'You've seen the Indians working in the fields that they've hacked out of your precious forest. Try telling them to think of the long term, when all their concern has to be with existing in the here and now. You can't feed babies and children with dreams.'

'Oh, quite the politician, aren't we?' she snarled, and was astonished to see fury, almost uncontrollable, flaring in his eyes, to be succeeded swiftly by a chilling hauteur.

'You are quite wrong there.' His voice was carefully controlled. 'As it happens, I take no interest whatsoever in politics.'

Despite the steel edge to his voice, she could not quite focus on him any longer, for whoever had been busily filling her head with straw had now finished and was starting on the rest of her body.

'What's the matter with you now?'

'What?' She winced as the face opposite her turned into four scowling faces, all gyrating in front of her. 'I—I'm quite all right.'

'I told you not to have that lager. You stubborn little fool——'

She wasn't staying here to be insulted. 'I—I'm going to bed,' she said, and got up with tremendous dignity.

The whole effect, though, was ruined when she had to put her hands hastily on the table to steady herself as she felt her scarecrow body very slowly begin to keel over towards it, exactly as though she were falling from some huge cliff.

Dimly, she heard someone push back a chair, then, just as she was laying her head comfortably down on the table, someone else dragged her to her feet. She mumbled irritably, trying to push them away, but they were stronger than she. She felt herself being lifted, struggled feebly for a moment, then surrendered, leaned back against something comfortingly warm and solid, and let herself tumble headlong over the cliff edge.

Cal half opened her eyes—to a white, all-enveloping mist. For a moment she lay, totally bewildered, then—of course . . . San Cristóbal . . . Chicambo . . . Pete's bungalow . . . her bedroom, where someone must have carefully draped the mosquito net around her narrow bed. She frowned, trying to bring into focus the previous evening, but it was no use. She could dimly remember standing by the kitchen table, then very slowly folding to her knees—and nothing more. But in that case that same someone must have carried her through to here, put her into bed and——

One corner of the net twitched suddenly and, beneath the sheet, she froze, but then a young girl, dark-eyed, black-haired, was looking down at her.

'Señorita Cal-yp-so?' She enunciated the word with great care, like a well-rehearsed lesson.

'Er—*sí*.' Cal smiled up at her, thinking. Oh lord, Spanish this early in the morning!

'How are you?' Still that cautious precision, but English, Cal thought gratefully.

'Oh, fine, thank you.'

And it was true—her head had lost that unnerving fuzziness, and even the unbearable pain in her arm had subsided to a low murmur. She sat up, hugging her wrap round her and feeling a little trickle of sweat run down her neck at the slight movement. The girl was still regarding her anxiously, and she smiled reassuringly at her again.

'Who are you?'

'My name is Rosa. Don Luis sent for me. He said you must not be left alone.'

Cal's horrified eyes took in the old bamboo chair, pulled up close beside her bed.

'You've been here all night? He really shouldn't——'

'Oh, no, *señorita*,' the girl cut in cheerfully. 'He stayed with you. I came only a few minutes ago.'

'Oh.' Cal tried to meet the frank interest in the brown eyes but, conscious that the colour was flooding her cheeks, she looked hastily down at the sheet.

'He said you are to stay in bed all day,' the girl went on firmly, a faint echo in her tone of that other, autocratic voice.

'Oh, did he?' said Cal grimly. 'Well, in that case——' ignoring the girl's horrified gasp, she pushed back the sheet and swung her legs to the floor '—I've got work to do, and the sooner I start, the better.'

Certainly, the sooner she was away from the house this morning, the better, she realised suddenly, for Revilla was quite capable of returning to ensure that his orders had been docilely obeyed. Really, she reflected, as she stood under the shower, for two people who'd obviously conceived such an instant mutual antipathy, they'd spent far too long in each other's company already.

The ride from the airport . . . his unexpected arrival last night and its humiliating aftermath . . . her collapse and then, she thought uneasily, his staying by her through the long watches of the night. What must he have thought of her as she'd lain, tossing and turning, muttering in that shallow twilight sleep she could just faintly recollect? Her mouth tightened. It must surely have confirmed his masculine prejudice that she was wholly unfit to be out here.

And then, suddenly, those vague, insubstantial memories jelled into solidity in her mind. Throughout those hours of heat and pain, there had been hands—cooling, soothing hands which had bathed her burning arm, wiped the drops of sweat from her clammy brow, and raised her to give her sips of water . . .

Very thoughtfully, she put on a white T-shirt and blue denim shorts and went through to the kitchen. Her breakfast had been set at one end of the table and Rosa was standing at the small stove stirring the contents of a saucepan.

'You like eggs?' She did not turn round.

'Oh, yes—scrambled, that's lovely,' Cal replied, then as she went to sit down she looked more closely at the girl. Her shoulders were hunched against the cotton of her skimpy dress, washy blue apart from a cake-frill of the original navy at the waist where the gathers had burst open.

'Is—is something wrong?' she asked gently, and was horrified when she heard a muffled sob. She put her arm round the thin shoulders and moved the saucepan off the heat.

'Please, Rosa, tell me—what is it?'

'Señor Pete—he is ill. And what shall I do?'

The last word was a wail and, as Cal stared at her, aghast, the girl buried her head against her chest. As Cal stood holding her, looking down at the glossy, neatly braided black head, she began to be very afraid. Surely—*surely* Pete hadn't . . . ? The girl could hardly be more than thirteen, a pathetic, bedraggled little scrap—and yet she herself had already had more than a frightening glimpse of the effect the tropics could have . . .

'Please, stop crying,' she said tremulously. 'Perhaps I can help, but I can't if you won't tell me.'

The wails subsided at last, and in a sob-drenched mixture of English, Spanish and an Indian dialect Rosa poured out her problem. As she pieced it together Cal's heart lifted in grateful relief. Pete, it seemed, employed the girl as his housekeeper and now, with him away and with a widowed mother and five younger brothers and sisters, she was very afraid that Cal wouldn't want her. She would be able to look after herself or—even worse—she might employ another girl.

All the same, Cal's purse was not exactly overflowing. 'Er—how much did he pay you?' she asked, rather nervously, but Rosa named what seemed such a ridiculously low figure that she was able to hug her and say, 'Oh, I think I can manage that. Now you're not to worry any longer—and, anyway, Señor Pete will be back very soon,' she added, mentally crossing her fingers. 'Now, how about that scrambled egg you promised me?'

As she ate, she pored over one of Pete's meticulously kept notebooks. They were filled with precise recordings of all the species and sub-species of fauna in the reserve—she was going to have to try to match them with similar details of the plant life.

But it was almost impossible to concentrate, for Rosa was cleaning the bathroom, chirping away like a small linnet at some haunting, tuneless melody, so that she finally gave in and pushed the books away. Would that everybody's problems could be sorted out so easily, she thought, and smiled wryly to herself.

In any case, just out there was the forest, waiting for her, and she couldn't wait any longer. Pinned above Pete's desk was a huge, detailed map and she studied it carefully. Here was the village and, yes, this must be the reserve where she would be working, clearly marked in red felt tip. What a pathetically tiny area it looked, just a minute segment, with the forest encircling it, stretching far away all round the inked outline. Was this what PET and all those other conservation groups round the world had campaigned for, put so much effort into raising funds for?

Her finger was still wandering across the stiff linen paper, towards—the Hacienda Palomita. That must be where——Angrily, she snatched her hand away and dragged her eyes back to the reserve. This was the stream at the back of the house. The red boundary line followed it, so if she used it as a marker she could be sure of not getting lost.

This morning would be just a preliminary reconnoitre while she got her bearings, so there was no need to load herself with all her surveying paraphernalia—just binoculars, small magnifying glass, camera, notebook and pencil. She packed them into a small, battered rucksack that lay beside the desk—Pete's, presumably, but much lighter than hers.

She changed into jeans, eyed her trainers regretfully, but then dutifully put on the boots she'd been told to bring. She knew that most snakes could be relied on to glide away from her unseen, but even so . . . She swallowed down a salt tablet, dabbed her nose hopefully with some of the lotion she had bought just prior to leaving, the latest in a long line of anti-freckle preparations, then saw, hanging from a nail on the door, a large straw hat. It would certainly offer much more protection than her own drill hat.

She hesitated, but, after all, she was using Pete's food and his rucksack, so what was the point of a minor crisis of conscience over his straw hat? She snatched it up, shouted '*Adiós*' to Rosa, and closed the anti-mosquito mesh front door behind her.

CHAPTER FOUR

A HUNDRED yards or so upstream there was a small pool where a cluster of Indian women, two with babies strapped tightly to their backs, were washing clothes, beating them fiercely against rocks, scrubbing them, then laying them on the grass to bleach. Only one answered Cal's smiling, '*Buenos días, señoras*'; the rest merely stared at her, their gaze not in the least unfriendly, just watchful and curious.

The stream curved in a great arc and soon the women were out of sight. Ahead of her, two butterflies danced in the dappled shade cast by the trees, then fluttered down on to an oleander bush. Small, brilliant blue wings—she didn't recognise them, and made a mental note to look them up in her reference book when she got back to the house, then forgot them as, over the next hour, her senses were bludgeoned by a myriad new sensations.

More butterflies, even more beautiful than the first; tiny, crimson-throated hummingbirds; green lizards whisking off the path ahead; a huge marching column of brown ants—Cal squatted on her haunches for several minutes watching them as they resolutely patrolled their dusty freeway. And all round her were the trees, their trunks encrusted with bright green mosses and grey, spidery lichens, while from every branch hung the twisted ropes of lianas.

It was very hot, and getting hotter by the second, so that she was beginning to feel as though her entire body had been immersed in a steam bath. She mopped her face; perhaps this was long enough for her first tentative foray. But just then she caught, far ahead, a flash of green and red. Parakeets—swarms of them, chattering argumentatively; even at that distance she could hear their indignant squawks.

She ran down the path in pursuit. There they were, just disappearing into a tangled thicket on the far side of the stream. A fallen tree bridged the water and, without stopping to think, she scrambled across it then clawed her way through the mass of weird-looking buttressed fig trees and bamboos which lined the bank.

But the birds had gone. One last flutter of wings, a distant shriek, then she was alone. She stood, looking slowly around her. She'd expected the forest to be full of noises—insects, birds, small mammals—but it was now absolutely silent, so that she could hear the beating of her heart as it thumped against her ribs.

The trees were huge, silver-trunked giants, the sunlight only penetrating their thick green canopies in tiny golden light-jewels far above her. It was almost as though she were in some immense, deserted cathedral. And yet she knew, with a sudden prickling of the hairs on her neck, that everywhere there were unseen watchers, a multitude of creatures that had seen her enter their hidden world.

Growing from some of the highest branches

were epiphytes, the strange air plants which eked out an insecure existence among the forest rooftops. One plant in particular caught her eye—a bromeliad certainly, but with enormous pink leaves, far bigger, surely, than any she'd seen described in her book on the flora of Central America. Could it possibly be a new variety, as yet undiscovered? Surely not? And yet . . . *Nidularium purpureum calypso wardii* . . . The words danced in front of her . . .

With shaking hands, she dug out her binoculars and focused them, but it was no use. There was only one way to make sure. The tree was no more difficult to climb than the ones at home which she'd regularly clambered up and fallen out of as a child. So, leaving her gear at the foot of the tree, she heaved herself up on to the lowest branch.

Ten minutes later, she was perched precariously on the branch above her quarry, her perspiring face puckered in disappointment. Oh, well, it was really too much to expect that on her very first day she should discover a brand new species, but really, not to have recognised *Aechmea fulgens discolor*. Thank goodness Pete wasn't with her!

She was just turning herself round gingerly to begin the tricky descent when she froze. Somewhere—not far away—something was blundering through the undergrowth. Cal, her throat suddenly chalky dry, gripped the branch convulsively, the rough bark scratching at her palms. Was it? No—jaguars didn't live on the fringes of the forest, but well in the interior, safe from men, didn't they? But there could always be a rogue one—and the big cats could climb trees, couldn't they?

She stared down through the screen of leaves, her breathing virtually suspended, but then, as two small pigs burst out of the bushes grunting indignantly, trotted across the clearing and disappeared, she almost laughed out loud at herself. Well, perhaps at least she was getting rid of all her naïveté in one morning.

Her relief was short-lived, though. Hardly had the pigs' blundering footsteps faded before there erupted into the clearing two huge animals. Cal, who had just lowered the toe of one foot to the next branch down, hastily lifted it again and stared down, horrified. They were dogs—mastiffs, black-muzzled and menacing—and they'd obviously been on the trail of the pigs.

But as she watched, peering down past her feet, she saw them pick up not the pigs' scent, but hers. Low growls rumbling from their massive chests, they tailed her first across the clearing towards the stream, then, as she silently willed them to go, they circled back and finally erupted in a volley of savage barks, leaping up at the tree.

Above the noise, Cal did not hear the new arrival. The first warning she had of his presence was when she caught a movement behind the dogs, and, parting the leaves stealthily, she glimpsed a man on a chestnut horse. So the dogs weren't wild, as she'd half feared. She let out a breath of relief, but then as he glanced up his face, which had been screened by a wide-brimmed black riding hat, became all too visible.

She let the leaves fall back into place and leaned against the trunk with a silent groan of misery. Of all the men in a twenty-mile radius, why, *why* did it have to be this one? Still, her rucksack was on the far side of the huge tree trunk, he hadn't seen it, and if she sat very still he would decide that all his dogs had done was flush out a parrot or a monkey and——

'Come down out of there.'

His voice was not raised, but it vibrated with anger, and Cal, not even breathing now, tried to shrink inside her skin.

'I said, come down. I know you're there.'

No, you don't, not really. If I keep absolutely still——

'I'll give you up to three.'

She lifted aside a tiny branchlet with one finger, then almost fell out of the tree. Thirty feet below her, Luis Revilla was lifting a light hunting rifle which had been jammed down alongside his saddle. As she stared down, she saw him snap the gun to and let it lie negligently along his right arm.

'One.'

He wouldn't dare—he simply wouldn't dare.

'Two.'

In the silence she distinctly heard the click as he cocked the weapon.

'Oh, all right. I'm coming!' she snarled, in a fair imitation of the mastiffs, and, loosening her grip, she carefully swung herself down to the next spreading bough. As she continued her reluctant descent, it suddenly registered that he had been speaking English. In which case, he must have recognised her from the first . . .

The toe-holds which she had found so easily on the way up had mysteriously disappeared, but at last she clawed her way down to the lowest branch, just above his head, though she still refused to look at him.

'Would you please move out of the way?'

She was gratified by the dignity in her voice, but then, as she turned to let herself down, the back of her jeans caught on a projecting branch and she overbalanced. Before she could do more than suck in her breath a pair of strong hands had snatched her, out of mid-air as it seemed, and brought her down in a tangled heap of arms and legs across the saddle in front of him.

As the horse snorted and pranced sideways under them, she made a clutch at him, at the same moment as his arms tightened instinctively to stop her falling. Their faces were very close, so close that his breath stirred the tendrils of tawny-blonde hair that lay damply across her forehead and she could see minute points of light, reflected off the latticed leaves overhead, sparking in his sooty-brown eyes, the edges of the long lashes dusted with gilt . . .

She drew back suddenly and lowered her eyes to his shirt, then saw with horror the marks of her filthy hands on the pristine white.

'Oh, I'm sorry,' she blurted out, and began futilely dabbing at the lichen stains, then stopped abruptly as she felt his warm, hard chest beneath her fumbling hands.

A gold medallion, a tiny, beautifully crafted

jaguar mask—lips drawn back in a snarl, jade eyes flashing cold fire—lay against the base of his throat, and she was almost sure that she could see beneath it the faint pulse of blood under the smooth, silky skin. She swallowed, almost mesmerised by that scarcely perceptible indication of the strong life force surging through that powerful body, then jerked her eyes away, just as he loosed his grip slightly, swung himself from the saddle and hauled her unceremoniously down beside him.

'What the hell do you think you're playing at?'

The fury in his voice made her insides turn to water momentarily, but then she rallied her strength and glared back at him.

'If you must know, I was looking at that air plant up there.' She gestured, but he did not look up. 'I suppose you're going to tell me that, as a mere woman, I shouldn't be climbing trees.'

'You can climb as many bloody trees as you like, or try to break your silly little neck as often as you want to, but not *my* trees, on *my* land.'

'*Your* land?' Her jaw sagged. 'It—it can't be. I checked the map; your hacienda is miles away—over there.'

'Sorry to disappoint you.' His voice rasped on her ears like sandpaper. 'I appreciate that it must be extremely painful for you to accept, but this is my land——' he paused '—all two hundred thousand hectares of it.'

She closed her eyes for a moment. Two hundred thousand . . . So their tiny sliver of land, that precious fragment, was just a grain of sand on this man's beach. How horribly unjust, that one man—the anger welled in her, but she forced it down. After all, she was, technically, in the wrong, and it would be extremely unwise to alienate him any further; she was beginning to realise, with a sinking heart, that far from being constantly tucked safely away on his plantation he could exert, if he chose to, an unpalatably powerful influence over her activities. He clearly detested all conservationists—and her in particular, to judge from the way he was scowling at her, exactly as though he was only keeping his hands off her with a tremendous effort. A grovelling apology was obviously needed.

'I'm sorry,' she muttered, then forced a placatory smile. 'I didn't realise. You see, I—I was following some birds and——'

His laugh was barely more than a sneer. 'Don't give me that crap.' She winced at the crudity. 'Sanderson would be really proud of you. Your first day and you can't keep your feet off my territory.'

Fury that he had flung her apology back in her face made her cast aside all her best resolutions. 'That's hardly surprising,' she flared, her topaz eyes flashing gold fire, 'considering how pitifully tiny our land is compared with yours.'

'Well, just be grateful my father was ill-advised enough to sell that much to you.'

'Your father?'

'Yes.' He regarded her grimly. 'But just because he allowed himself to fall for Sanderson's persuasive tongue, don't go getting any ideas that his son is going to follow in his misguided footsteps.'

'You mean—let us have more of your land?' Sudden enlightenment dawned. 'So that's what you and Pete have been fighting about.'

'Got it in one.'

'But why won't you?'

'I told you yesterday. I have a duty to the people on my land—my people——'

'Your people? Oh, spare me the enlightened despot act, please,' she said scornfully, and his brows came down thunderously. 'It's nothing to do with the people. It's simply that you haven't the slightest intention of giving up one square centimetre of your land.'

He took a threatening step towards her, but she stood her ground. 'Of course the Indians have got to be protected, and of course some of the timber has to be cut down, I know that, but it can be done properly—coppiced so that new growth can start, not just destroyed forever.'

His lips tightened impatiently, but she swept on, a vision of a better—larger—Chicambo Reserve blazing in her mind like a pyrotechnic display. 'If only we had more land, Chicambo needn't be just a study centre—it could be a living model of how a rain forest should be managed. Look, let me show you.'

She squatted down and, snatching up a piece of dry twig, swept the sandy ground clear of debris. Frowning in concentration as she tried to recall the map above Pete's desk, she began to make a lightning sketch.

'Here's the village . . . the stream . . . the boundary—*your* boundary. Now, if you were to let us have this piece of land here . . .' She glanced up at him, but his face was expressionless, then she added hurriedly, 'Of course, we'd pay the full market price for it.' Another campaign for PET. Perhaps she could start to organise it from here. 'We wouldn't expect you to give it to us.'

'That's remarkably generous of you.'

'And then, with that much land, we could divide it into different zones, like they're doing in Costa Rica. You know—this part to carry on the scientific research——' a rapid squiggle of the twig '—this part for forestry——' another squiggle '—and this for the public to visit. Tourism could really take off, and that would bring in more income for the people. It could be San Cristóbal's very first national park—we could get the government involved, and ——'.

'No!'

A well-polished riding boot came down, scraping the tips of her fingers, and viciously ground out the little map. As she sat back on her heels to stare up at him, he said, 'You're forgetting just one thing, Señorita Ward. This is my land you're so busy appropriating, and, I'll tell you for free, you won't get it, not in a thousand years.'

Very slowly, she stood up, automatically rubbing her dusty hands down her jeans, while he stood regarding her, flicking his whip against his boot. She tried to meet his cold, angry gaze unflinchingly, but it was no use. He was the only man, she thought involuntarily, that she'd ever met who made her feel positively tiny. Not so much because, tall though she was, he was head and shoulders taller, but there was—*something* in his personality, something which was threatening to dominate her in a wholly new way, and she knew, with a sudden frightening conviction, that if she did not shake herself free it could completely overwhelm her.

She was about to bend down for her rucksack when the two mastiffs came bounding back into the clearing. They made straight for her and she flinched away for a moment, but they merely thrust their cold noses at her, and when she tentatively put her hand on one of the glossy, wrinkled foreheads the animal's wet tongue slobbered all over it.

'Oh, they're beautiful.' She looked up at Revilla and added, 'I was absolutely terrified when they appeared, but they're just a pair of old softies.'

'I wouldn't bank on it,' he responded drily. 'They'd be more than willing to take you apart at the seams if I gave them the command.'

'Oh, then it's as well you're not going to,' she replied lamely.

'Don't tempt me, honey,' He snapped his fingers peremptorily and the dogs retreated instantly to sit on their haunches, watching him.

Cal picked up her rucksack, jammed the straw hat down over her ears and turned to go.

'Did Rosa not pass on my instructions?'

'What? Oh—oh, yes,' she said hastily, fearful that the next thunderbolt would fall on the girl's innocent head. 'But I felt so much better this morning, I couldn't possibly stay in bed, not with all this——' she waved her arm around expansively, then amended hastily '—at least, not *this*, but all Chicambo, just waiting for me.'

She looked up at him again, conscious that something of the excitement of the morning must have still glowed irrepressibly in her face, but he merely regarded her unsmilingly for several seconds before saying, 'Your arm—is it better?'

'Oh, much, thank you.'

She flexed it to show him, but then, before she could draw back, he had caught hold of her wrist with one hand, and with the other was folding back the sleeve of her T-shirt. Very gently, he brushed his fingers across her skin and instantly that same strange, flickering sensation which she'd felt the previous evening rippled through her again, making her want to swallow hard and, at the same time, breathe in deep gulps of air.

He was studying her arm intently and she shot him a covert look. His face still wore that habitual mask of cold indifference and yet—how strained he looked. Yesterday she'd thought it was simply the result of fatigue, but the lines were still there today, etched deep in the dark, tanned skin . . . round the eyes, the mouth . . . a horizontal cleft between the black brows . . .

She sensed, all at once, that he was a man who needed constantly to hold himself under iron control. But the thought did not frighten her. Rather, she was suddenly filled with the desire to reach up her hand and softly smooth away those marks of strain, to hold him in her arms and say,

'Don't look like that—please, don't'.

The appalling, treacherous thought sent a tidal shock wave through her, and he must have sensed the tremor for he asked, 'Am I hurting you?'

'N—no,' she said huskily, but could not quite meet his eye.

'Hmm. Well, it's much better. You must be tougher than you look. Stubborn, foolhardy, but definitely tough.'

For one magic, fleeting moment there was a faint warmth in his eyes and, aware that beneath her freckles the hot colour was staining her cheeks peony-pink, she said hurriedly, 'I—I haven't thanked you for staying with me.'

He shrugged. 'Well, you obviously need someone to look after you—full time, on present performance.'

She felt herself colour even more and, conscious of his eyes studying her intense blush with clinical interest, said jerkily, 'I just can't make you out, you know. You obviously loathe Pete—and me as well—yet you saved his life yesterday. Yes, you did,' as he gestured dismissively, 'and then you looked after me last night. No, I just can't understand you,' she finished, shaking her head.

'Oh, it's quite simple,' he said carelessly. 'If I were to come across a dangerous animal—a jaguar, say—wounded, out here in the forest, I'd do what I could for it.'

'So that's how you see us—as dangerous animals?'

'Of course.' He paused, then went on slowly, 'I didn't figure it out at first, but I'm just beginning

to realise that you're going to be every bit as cussed
as ever Sanderson was.' He eyed her reflectively.
'And maybe more so. I had more than enough of
your company yesterday, and I can't come out
riding this morning without tripping over you.
You're already a nuisance, and I have an
unpleasant suspicion that unless you're kept firmly
under control you'll rapidly develop into a pest,
and from a pest to a goddam pain in the backside.'

Before Cal could even draw in an indignant
breath, he had snatched at his horse's bridle.
'Come on, I'll see you off my territory.'

'Oh, there's no need!' she snapped. 'I know the
way.'

'Maybe, but I prefer to satisfy myself that you've
really gone.'

At the stream, she sat down and began pulling
off her boots.

'What the hell are you doing now?'

'I don't want to get them wet, of course,' she said
briefly, and tugged off a sock.

'Don't be such a fool!' he shouted, then shook
his head in exasperation. 'It's true—you really do
need a permanent nursemaid. Didn't they tell you
that you should never wade through water here in
bare feet?'

Just for a moment, she glanced at the river
flowing past her, half expecting to see a pair of evil
jaws snapping, but the green water sparkled
innocuously under the dappled sunlight, for all the
world like an English stream.

'I suppose you're going to tell me there's a shoal
of man-eating piranhas just waiting to get their

teeth into me.'

With great deliberation, she pulled off the second sock and stood up, then a moment later gave a yell of angry surprise as, with a smothered curse, he snatched her up and, holding her wriggling body under one arm like a sack of potatoes, splashed out into the stream. Totally ignoring her struggles and muffled imprecations, he dumped her unceremoniously on the far bank, then stood regarding her, breathing hard.

'Next time I tell you to do something, *do it*! All the rivers here are full of leeches—bloodsucking leeches. I was sorely tempted to let them get stuck into you—it might even have taught you a lesson you obviously need. But you, no doubt, would have been begging me to get them out for you, and I just can't spare any more time for stupid little PETs today.'

'Oh, you—you——'

She was still struggling to find the most satisfying word when he turned and waded back to the opposite bank. A second later her boots came hurtling across the ribbon of water.

'And remember, Señorita Ward—keep off my land, and keep away from me.' Calling his dogs to heel, he swung himself up into the saddle and rode off through the trees.

She finally found the word she'd been ransacking her brain for and flung it several times in the direction he had taken, in a wholly unsuccessful attempt to relieve her sizzling temper.

CHAPTER FIVE

'FINISHED!'

Cal inked in the final twirl of the exotic orchid petal, carefully rubbed out the pencil lines, then sat back, pushing the heavy fringe away from her clammy forehead.

She surveyed the drawing with satisfaction; it had taken her most of the afternoon, but now—here it was, captured in the large loose-leafed file which was rapidly filling up with her botanical notes and diagrams. Beautiful yellow flowers, like enormous graceful spiders . . . she'd come across it quite by chance in the forest, taken photographs and made rough sketches. She wrote *'Epidendrum Cochleatum'* neatly underneath, then put her pen down and idly flicked through the pages.

That flamingo flower—*Anthurium scherzerianum*. She'd found that in her first week, its vivid scarlet blazing from among the soft greens of the surrounding undergrowth; and then those pretty flame-violets—she remembered the morning she'd found a whole colony, hundreds of the small red-starred plants growing over a huge, rotting tree stump.

She flexed her aching hands, swivelled her chair back on one leg, and lifted out from the fridge behind her the jug of iced lime water which Rosa had made for her that morning. She gulped down

70

a glass, then tried to settle to work again, but her attention would keep straying to that gap in the almost-closed shutters through which she could just see the huge grey trunk of a silk cotton tree, its leaves rustling stiffly in the hot breeze, and beyond that the edge of the forest.

This house ... the forest ... the village—these had become so much her world that it seemed quite impossible that she'd been here scarcely more than a month. Everything before that had become a vague dream: her flat ... her job ... Phil—

Phil. She smiled rather ruefully to herself. A trip to Chicambo could definitely be recommended as a sure-fire cure for a badly broken heart—except that she knew now that she hadn't even been suffering from a bruised, never mind broken, heart; only her pride had been badly dented for a while. She'd never loved him—she'd realised that weeks ago—and surely he'd never loved her. So completely different, perhaps it was a simple case of opposites attracting.

Even so, what had they ever seen in one another? True, he was charming, fun to be with, very good-looking—and yet now, when she screwed up her eyes, she couldn't even see his face any more. Blue eyes ... dark brown hair ... straight nose. She tried to assemble the pieces, but it was no use, Phil's handsome face simply would not jell in her mind—or rather, she realised with a jolt, each time she struggled to focus on it another face *would* keep sliding across it, like a cloud across the moon, obscuring it in darkness——

'Hi there, Cal.'

She jerked back to reality as a shadow passed over her closed eyelids, then relaxed at the sound of Father Aidan's voice. He dug in his shirt pocket, brought out two flimsy airmail letters and dropped them in front of her. She snatched them up.

'Oh, great. One from home and,' she turned the blue envelope over, 'one from Libby, my best friend. Thanks, Father.'

'It's nothing. The post office was on my way to the hospital.'

He sat down and poured himself a glass of lime water.

'And Pete, how is he? Did you give him my note?'

'Yes, I did. He said thanks, and sorry again for the bother he's caused you.'

'Does he know yet when he's coming back?' Soon, I hope, she thought. Although she was enjoying the work immensely, without an expert to guide her she did worry sometimes whether she was doing everything just as she should. The group of students who'd been up from the university a couple of weeks back to help out had been great, but even so . . .

'Well, Cal, I'm afraid he isn't—at least, not for some time.' Cal bit back the exclamation of dismay. 'They're still rather concerned about that skull fracture and think he ought to go back to the States for more specialised treatment, so he's being flown home on Friday.'

'Oh, poor Pete.' Cal let out her breath in a shaky gust.

'Don't worry. He'll be all right, I'm sure—he's tough, that one, tough and wiry. No, it's you I'm concerned about, having to stay on here by yourself. I saw Luis yesterday and he told me,' Cal's lips tightened mutinously, 'that he offered to get you back home and you . . .' He paused.

'Well, go on,' she said, a shade defensively.

'He informed me,' the faintest smile was lurking in his blue eyes, 'that you were a little spitfire, more trouble than any woman he'd had the misfortune to meet up with and, as a mere male, he simply couldn't understand why you refused to take sensible advice and go home.'

'I'm sure he couldn't.' she said tartly.

'Hmm. Have you seen him lately?'

She shook her head. 'No.'

In fact, that was not the absolute truth. Since that abrasive encounter on her first morning, she'd taken good care to obey his parting injunction, however much it still rankled in her mind. She hadn't come face to face with him, but that was only because she'd used every possible avoidance tactic—hastily retreating or ducking out of sight on several occasions when she'd seen him talking to Father Aidan or some of the villagers. Once, as she'd sidled behind a clump of bushes, she'd been almost sure that he'd caught sight of her, but he'd immediately turned his head away, obviously no more anxious to see her than she him.

The priest's eyes were taking in her sun-reddened arms and shoulders, the insect bites, several of which had turned septic when she'd scratched at them. Standing on the table was her freckle remover, which was turning out to be even more ineffectual than all the previous ones, and she saw him eyeing it, his lips twitching surreptitiously.

'Would you like me to have a word with him?'

Cal felt a sudden surge of irritation at the way these two men, however well intentioned one of them at least might be, *would* insist on viewing her as a totally helpless female.

'No, thank you, Father,' she said firmly. 'I came out here to do a job. Maybe with Pete not around, I shan't do it as well as I might have done, but I'll do my best, all the same. I'm not going home until I've finished—and you can tell that to—to anyone who asks——'

She broke off, feeling that she'd been rather abrupt, but he only said mildly, 'You don't like Luis, do you?'

'Well, I ——' his directness had taken her aback '—I don't really know him.'

But he was not fooled. 'Don't judge him too harshly, my dear. You're young, resilient, and you still have your high ideals intact. Luis is older, thirty-five, and he's lived much more than you. Besides,' he hesitated, 'he's a man who's seen his ideals—cruelly destroyed.' He stood up abruptly, but then turned back to Cal, who was still trying to assimilate his words. 'If you insist on staying, you must at least give yourself a break. You've been working in that forest or shut up in here all day and every day.' He shook his head in mock admonition. 'Don't forget—even the good Lord rested on the seventh.'

'Yes, maybe you're right. Perhaps I ought to take a day off.' A thought struck her. 'I've been reading about that ruined pre-Colombian city—Cueltazan—you know, way out in the forest. I'd love to see that before I leave, so now that Pete's Jeep has been repaired I could go there.'

The priest pursed his lips for a moment, but said nothing, and she followed him out to where his old motorbike stood. At that same moment a Land Rover roared round the corner; the driver braked, then seemed to be accelerating away again, until Father Aidan waved him to a reluctant halt.

As he jumped down and sauntered slowly towards them, his hands in his jeans pockets, Cal made an instinctive move back towards the house, but the priest caught her by the arm and she was forced to watch Revilla approaching, all too conscious that a most peculiar feeling, as though she had swallowed a myriad of those dazzling blue butterflies, had taken hold of her.

She was favoured with one cool nod of bare recognition, then, 'I was hoping to see you, Father. Are you on your way home?' he added pointedly.

'Yes, I am. Oh, and I'm glad I've seen you, Luis. Would you do me a great favour?'

'Of course, anything. What is it?'

'You know the ruins of Cueltazan?'

'Sure. You want me to take you? No problem.'

'No, not me. This young lady here was telling me that she's very keen to go.'

Cal, who had just mumbled a goodbye and was turning away, was suddenly rooted to the spot with horror. In spite of herself, her eyes flew to Revillas's face, and she saw his mouth tighten with anger, as though furious with himself at having been so neatly snared.

Just for a second he hesitated, then said smoothly, 'Of course, Father; I'd be delighted.' But he didn't look at her, and the faint flush of colour along the high line of his cheekbones betrayed his inner fury.

'Now, when would you like to go, Cal?' The priest was prompting her.

'Well, I—I'm not sure. Whenever would be convenient to Don Luis.'

He regarded her as though she'd just crawled out from under a wet leaf, then said flatly, 'Tomorrow?'

Of course. He wanted to get his ordeal over as soon as possible. 'That would be fine, thank you. That is, if you really don't mind.'

He ignored her last remark, as unworthy of notice. 'Be early. I shall want to make a start by daybreak—it'll be a long day. And wear sensible clothes—it's a higher altitude there.'

His cold gaze dropped for a moment to her turquoise cotton T shirt, boldly proclaiming, 'I'm a PET—join me', and his lips curled with a distaste which even Father Aidan's presence could not wholly subdue. Then he said, 'Now, if you'll excuse me, Father, I need to see Cornelio about housing the workmen when they get here, so I'll come on to you later.'

They watched as he drove off, then the priest remarked casually, 'That'll be about the electricity.

Luis is funding a big scheme to connect Chicambo to the national grid.'

'Oh.' Funding a big scheme for Chicambo? Could they possibly be talking about the same man?

'Yes. Of course, technically, since his father sold the land, he has no responsibility for this area, but he still takes an interest in the village. He's also setting up a school for the youngsters.'

'Is he?' Cal said politely. But she was thinking, with alarm, I don't want him to be like that. A grasping, avaricious predator was relatively easy to cope with—he fitted into his slot neatly—but a caring, philanthropic landowner—that was altogether different . . . She felt the mental image she'd created of Revilla begin to shift, even crack a little. She remembered her cheap jibe—'Oh, spare me the enlightened despot act,'—and winced. Why on earth hadn't he put her right? Too proud, of course—and totally indifferent to how she viewed him.

She watched Father Aidan in silence as he settled himself on his motorbike. 'Good. That's settled the little problem of your trip then.'

He smiled at her, apparently serenely oblivious of the invisible cross-currents which had been swirling around his head for the last few minutes, started up the machine and rode off.

Be early, he'd said. Cal glanced down at the luminous hands of her watch and hoped that five a.m. was early enough. The headlights of the Jeep lit up the discreet white board proclaiming

Hacienda Palomita, and she swung off the road between two high gateposts and began the long, gentle ascent, the track bordered on each side by plantations of cacao plants.

After three or four miles these were replaced by an avenue of elegant palm trees, then the drive widened to a graceful sweep of gravel, and the hacienda was before her. Although it was still dark, she could make out the elegant lines of a single-storey, colonial-style building, white-walled, with wrought-iron balconies, and with most of its wooden shutters still closed.

Revilla's Land Rover was already parked outside and, in a sudden fit of bravado designed to quell the tremors, not exactly of fear, but of nervous excitement, that were rippling through her, she pulled up just half a hair's breadth behind it. She lifted out her bag, took a deep breath and walked up the imposing flight of stone steps to the front entrance.

She tugged at the brass bell-pull and after a few moments she heard footsteps, then the door was flung open and Revilla was facing her. He was wearing a black robe which reached to just below his knees; his feet were thrust into black espadrilles, but his tanned legs were bare . . . Hastily, she raised her eyes to his face. It was still dark and the light from the hall was behind him, but she was very sure that he was not returning her artificially bright smile. She ran her tongue round the edge of her lips.

'I—er—hope I'm not too early.' When he did not reply, she added, 'You did say by daybreak.'

Without a word, he stood back and motioned her past him. The huge hall was paved with a mosaic of black and white tiles, and as he led the way across it she registered fleetingly the white-painted panelled walls and the old, highly polished dark wooden chests, the only splashes of colour coming from vivid, Spanish-style fringed rugs.

He continued down a passage and into the kitchen, where a huge black wood-burning range was glowing in one corner. A hastily pushed-back chair stood by a table on which were the remains of a breakfast. She felt his eyes on her, then he said abruptly, 'Have you eaten?'

'Er, not exactly. In fact, to be honest, I was terrified of being late, and in any case I was just too excited to eat.'

She smiled up at him candidly, something of her eager anticipation shining through her glowing face, but he only regarded her for a moment then said brusquely, 'In that case, sit down and have something to eat.'

'Oh, no, really,' she protested. 'I'm not hungry—honestly.'

'Either you eat, or you don't come. I'm not having you fainting on me before we even get there.'

As he strode across to a dresser to take out a cup and a plate she aimed a dagger of pure hatred straight at his shoulder-blades which should have felled him at twenty metres, but then, as he pulled out a second chair, she meekly subsided into it.

He poured orange juice from a jug and placed

it in front of her, then reached over the table to
slide across a basket of freshly baked brioches and
two dishes of butter and honey. As he sat down
opposite her and poured himself a cup of steaming
chocolate she raised her eyes to look at him, then
swiftly lowered them again to give all her attention
to spreading butter with meticulous care on her
roll.

He had obviously showered before eating: his
hair was damp, the edges of his black robe had
fallen apart to reveal the light sprinkling of tiny
black curls across his chest, and she caught the
musky scent of sandalwood. He was, she was
certain, naked beneath the robe.

'Chocolate?'

'Oh, yes, thank you.'

He leaned across to pour her a cup and she took
a sip of the rich, creamy liquid.

'Mmm, it's delicious. Is this from your own
plantation?'

'Yes.'

'You know, I've really acquired a taste for it. I
don't think I'll ever be able to go back to boring
old coffee again. I'll have to look out for San
Cristóbal chocolate when I get back to London.'

'Uh huh.' It was no more than a grunt.

She tried to push down her growing irritation.
She knew that her conversation was beginning to
veer towards the inane, but that was only because
of her quite understandable inner tension, and he
was making no effort at all to put her at her ease.

She made up her mind not to speak again until
he did, but finally, her nerves strained almost to

splintering point by his morose silence, she said abruptly, 'Look, I know you think that I got Father Aidan to ask you to take me out, but——'

He laughed shortly. 'Actually, you're wrong. On this occasion at least I'm prepared to give you the benefit of the doubt.'

'Well, that's big of you.'

'Yes, Father Aidan's perfectly capable of thinking up devious schemes for my intended well-being wholly unaided.'

Cal was not at all sure what to make of this ambiguous remark, but at least Revilla was talking, so she ventured to another tack. 'I've had a look at the map, but I can't see any road leading to Cueltazan. It must be a pretty rough track if it's not even shown.'

He shrugged carelessly. 'You'll see.'

'The ruins—are they on your land?'

'Yes, they are.'

His tone was barely civil and seemed to be implying, Do you want to make anything of it? At last her self-control snapped and she set down her cup with a bang.

'Look, I know you detest me and everything about me, and that the last thing you want is to have me foisted on you yet again. But you did agree to take me, and if we *are* going to spend the day together the least you can do is make an effort to be slightly civil. And if you can't, well, you damn well needn't bother. I'll go on my own, as I was planning to do in the first place.'

She raised her eyes to see his reaction, but his face was totally without expression, so she lowered hers again to her plate. 'I was really looking forward to seeing Cueltazan—I've read so much about it. If you must know, I c-could hardly sleep last night, I was so excited, but you're quite determined to ruin it for me, so let's just forget it.'

She pushed back her chair, but before she could get up he was round the table to her. He put both hands on her shoulders to force her back down, and when she tried to twist from under him his grip tightened.

'Sit still.'

His voice was gentle, but he did not loosen his hold until she grudgingly obeyed. Then he looked down at her and rested his hand on her head for a moment.

'OK, you're right. I guess I'm just never at my amiable best at five in the morning.' His features softened momentarily into a disarming, self-deprecating smile. 'Now, you finish your breakfast, *queridita*, and I'll be with you in ten minutes.'

Her hand was trembling slightly as she raised her cup; she buttered the last brioche mechanically and ate it without tasting its delicious feathery richness. At least he hadn't hurled her sudden outburst of temper back in her face, but she would, she reflected, have coped far more easily with that than with the mercurial change of mood it had provoked. *Queridita*, that term of endearment, and, even more, that sudden, magical smile—so rare in this man, she was sure—which had made her feel as though she'd just been gently sandbagged in the solar plexus, had knocked her off balance far more than yet more of his snarls would ever have done.

She was still toying with her cup when he came back. She glanced up and saw that he was now wearing jeans and a chunky cream sweater. To her astonishment, he was carrying two black leather flying jackets and he tossed one across to her.

'Right, get into this.'

'Oh, it's all right, thanks. I'm warm enough in this.'

She indicated her fleecy sweatshirt, then, as she saw his eyes travel slowly over it, went on, a shade belligerently, 'I hope it meets with your approval.'

After all, she'd spent several anxious moments the previous evening riffling through her meagre wardrobe to choose her most inoffensive garment. Surely even he could not take exception to this plain white shirt with its discreet, minuscule PET logo?

'Don't worry,' he said slowly. 'I was only asking myself just what kind of a blind fool I was ever to have taken you for a boy.'

'Oh.' The feeble response was all she could manage, for, once again, he had completely disconcerted her.

'Now, do as I say, and put it on.'

He shrugged himself into his jacket, and without another word she put hers on. She was struggling with the heavy metal zip when he lifted her hands clear.

'Here—let me do that.'

As he pulled up the zip his fingers brushed against her chin and, for a second, their eyes met.

Then his lips tightened. 'Come on. We've wasted enough time.' And he strode off down the passage, leaving her to hurry after him.

To her surprise, he led her past the Land Rover, round to the side of the house, where a small blue-and-white helicopter was parked on a circular concrete landing-pad.

'Are we going in *that*?' The last word was a squeak.

He glanced at her briefly. 'Sure. After all, as you said yourself, there aren't any roads to Cueltazan.'

He took her bag out of her hands, which had suddenly gone rigid, and motioned her to climb in. He slid her door to, then swung himself in beside her, fixing the seat-belt around her so adroitly that, whether deliberately or by accident she wasn't sure, he managed to avoid touching her at any point, then buckled himself in. Above her, the rotor blade turned, the engine roared into powerful life and the ground dropped away beneath them.

'What?'

He was saying something to her, but she didn't turn.

'I said, you can open your eyes.'

Swivelling round, she realised that he'd been fully aware of her screwed-up eyes, and no doubt also of her clenched hands clutching at the seat.

As she flushed with embarrassment, he shouted, 'Look!'

Reluctantly, she allowed her eyes to follow his pointing finger, and then she gasped. They must have been flying due east, for ahead of them the

sun was just rising from behind a distant ridge of
mountains, jagged-edged as though they had been
hacked from black paper. The rim showed copper
first, changing to red-gold as it slid up into the sky,
turning it into a strange translucent green.

'It's beautiful—marvellous!'

She tried to yell above the roar, but then just
smiled and shook her head. If only she could hold
it in her hands forever—but that unearthly, limpid
green was already fading to ordinary blue, while
below them the forest was lighting up under the
first rays of the sun.

For the rest of the flight Cal sat forward in her
seat, looking down at the green, billowing sea of
treetops beneath them, and then, after about half
an hour, she saw that directly ahead the land fell
away to a valley, completely encircled by the
mountains. Straining her eyes, she could make out
an open space in the forest from which a group of
stone buildings rose as though from the green
foam.

They were descending now, skimming the tops
of the trees like water-skiers, then as they hovered
above the clearing Revilla studied the ground
closely, finally gave a grunt of satisfaction, and
seconds later they had touched down.

CHAPTER SIX

HE cut the engine and the rotor blades died with a whine, then, as he jumped down and came round to Cal's side, she scrambled out, ignoring his outstretched hand.

'It's all right. I can manage, thanks.' She didn't want him to think for an instant that he had to look after her today, as well as bringing her, although she could see now how impossible it would have been for her to get here on her own.

He had pulled off his flying jacket so she took off hers, and he tossed them on to the rear seats of the helicopter as she stood staring around her, her breath quickening in anticipation. They were in an enormous rectangular clearing, the centre of which was paved, although most of the slabs were broken and weeds grew up everywhere through the cracks.

Facing them was a long, low building, its doorways hard black lozenges against the grey, weathered stone. Other, smaller buildings lined the central area, like a city plaza, except that all around them the forest was pressing in at their backs. At the far end was a massive stepped pyramid, its façade crumbling like a huge, mildewed wedding-cake; even at this distance Cal could see the ruined masonry, and young trees and bushes sprouting out from where their seeds had found minute toe-holds.

'Well, what do you think of Cueltazan then?' He was watching her face intently.

'It—it's wonderful.' She fumbled for her words. 'It's the most amazing place I've ever seen.'

He was still watching her, his brows drawn down into a faint frown, so that all at once she had the feeling that he wasn't really hearing anything she said, but then he shrugged.

'Oh, there are much better preserved places than this—in Mexico, for instance. If you went to Teotihuacán or Uxmal, all this would seem no big deal.'

'Yes, it would.' She shook her head firmly. 'And you think so too.'

Her vehemence seemed to take him aback, but then he nodded. 'You're right. I guess I get more of a kick out of this place each time I come.'

'I can see why,' she said seriously. 'It's so—oh, I don't know—sad, with the forest lapping at it, and yet it's so dignified. You have the marvellous feeling that the people have only just gone away for a while, and then they'll be back.'

She gave him a glowing smile and, in a spontaneous gesture, held out her hand. 'Thank you for bringing me, Don Luis.'

After a momentary hesitation, he reached out and took it, staring down at her slim, fine-boned hand as it lay in his large, callused palm, a strange unreadable expression on his unsmiling face, so that she almost feared she'd angered him, but he only said, 'My pleasure. And please, not Don Luis. Everyone calls me Luis, so that may as well include you—even if you are an obstinate, pig-headed PET.'

Just for a second, he grinned at her, but then, as she stared up at him, startled, he abruptly dropped her hand and strode away down the plaza, his booted feet ringing on the pavement.

When she caught up with him he was sprawled on the bottom step of the pyramid, his long legs stretched out in front of him, picking at a small plant which grew from a crack beside him and staring into the middle distance. She was beginning to get used to his abrupt changes of mood, even if she couldn't understand them, and she realised that he had retreated behind his blank wall again, slamming the door against her; she could almost feel his powerful personality repelling her. That first morning, she'd trespassed on his land; today, she felt uneasily that she was an unwelcome trespasser on his mind. But she would not let him shut that door completely—not today.

She plumped herself down beside him. 'What are those?'

Her tone was artificially bright and he glanced first at her before looking at where she was pointing. A row of tall stone tablets was propped up against the shell of a nearby building; strange figures with feathered heads and grotesque, grinning masks had been deeply incised in them.

'They're called stelae. The archaeologists found them scattered around the place and put them here. There are all sorts of crazy theories about their significance, but they probably had something to do with religion.'

She fished her camera out of her bag. 'Please, will you stand by them—so that people can see just how big they are?'

He uncoiled himself and leaned against the wall between the two middle stelae, his arms folded, gazing at her impassively. She took several shots, then, as she stared into the viewfinder, she thought, In a few weeks' time, this is all I shall have of him forever. The image blurred for an instant, then she blinked rapidly and it cleared.

'Finished?'

'Y-yes, thanks,' she said, but then, just as he was turning away, she took one last, surreptitious shot, his head and shoulders filling the entire frame.

As she came up to him he had his back to her, looking up at the precipitous side of the pyramid. He peeled off his sweater, dropped it on to the bottom step, and began tucking his white short-sleeved shirt into his jeans. That hard-muscled back . . . those strong shoulders under the fine cotton . . . He swung round and, all at once, she felt the power emanating from him—wholly unconscious, but no less potent for that, even though, as she increasingly sensed, it was kept under a ruthless, iron-willed control. She ran the top of her tongue around her lips, which had suddenly become dry, and thought, Supposing one day that ice-cold composure should crack—what then?

She felt a trickle of sweat on her back and, unable to risk meeting his eye, she replaced her camera in her bag and eased herself out of her sweatshirt, making very sure that her strawberry-pink T-shirt stayed in place as she did so.

'Can I climb the pyramid?' she asked. 'I won't damage it, will I?'

'I shouldn't think so—but I don't recommend it. The steps are very narrow, and they're crumbling dangerously in places.'

'Oh, I'll be very careful, I promise.'

He laughed shortly. 'I guess danger was the last thing I should have mentioned if I didn't want you to go up. Come on, then.'

He held out his hand, then, when she hesitated, he said with a hint of impatient finality, 'Either you hold my hand, or you don't go up there at all.' So she obediently took it.

The steps were even steeper than she'd realised from the ground, so that when she glanced up the grey stone stretched away above them like a cliff-face. They were very narrow too, so that she was forced to ascend slightly crooked, crabwise.

'They must have had very small feet—the people who built it,' she panted. Just then a piece of stonework rocked under her precariously and she gasped with fear, but his grip tightened and he hauled her up beside him.

'Please—stop a minute.' She was gulping for breath.

'We're almost there.'

'No, please—I must.'

She pulled on his hand and brought them to a standstill, then thrust her free hand to her side, where the sharp knife-thrust of stitch was cutting through her.

'Phew, that's better.'

Her heartbeat was settling down and she saw, only just above them, the level summit. She half turned, heard him say sharply, 'No, don't look down,' and glimpsed, far below her, the ground. She was like a fly on a perpendicular surface—if she put just a foot out into the air, she might——

She felt herself swaying slightly and he strengthened his hold on her, almost dragging her up the final steps, then caught her round the waist with both hands and swung her right off the ground, away from the almost sheer drop. He held her to him for a moment, then slowly released her.

'Sorry.' She gave a shaky laugh. 'Just for a second, it reminded me of the mountain in Wales where I did a lot of abseiling last summer. Ugh—it was horrible.' She gave him a shamefaced smile. 'I think I must be slightly prone to vertigo.'

'What a strange kid you are.' He was regarding her curiously. 'Climbing mountains—and *trees*,' he added meaningfully, 'and now this place. If you don't like climbing, why the hell do you do it? Are you trying to prove something, or what?'

'No, I don't think so,' she replied slowly. 'It's just that—well, you have to meet things that scare you head on, don't you?'

'Do you?' he asked drily.

'Yes.' She nodded fervently. 'Otherwise you just get more frightened of them. Oh, I don't know, it's——' She broke off.

'Tell me.' He raised his brows enquiringly.

'Well, for example, some huge brown rats live under the house back in Chicambo.' She shivered. 'I'm terrified of them, and when I first came I didn't dare go outside at night, but I couldn't let them make me a prisoner—some of the plants I'm studying open up at night—so now I make a lot of noise—and just pray they aren't stone deaf.'

She grinned at him, but he did not return her smile, so she went on, 'I don't like snakes either—not that I've seen one yet, thank goodness, but I always carry a stick when I'm out in the forest, just in case. There are some enormous dead ones hanging up in plastic bags in Pete's bedroom—and sometimes I have nightmares about them. I even woke up yelling my head off one night, convinced that they were crawling up the leg of my bed.'

She wrinkled her nose up. 'Of course, I don't know why I'm telling you all this. It'll just confirm all your worst prejudices, won't it?'

'Maybe,' he said briefly. 'Anyway, now you're up here, you'd better have a look round.'

In the centre of the platform there was a small stone building with no windows, just a stark doorway, so low that she had to duck under it, then she stood allowing her eyes to get used to the half-light after the tropical brilliance outside.

'Can you see?' She hadn't been aware that he had followed her in, until she felt his warm breath on her neck.

She peered into the gloom. 'Not really. What's that?'

Dimly, shapes were beginning to grow up in front of her, and when he fetched a small pocket-torch out of his jeans pocket and flicked it on she stared in amazement at what its pale beam revealed.

Along all four walls a wide frieze had been painted. The edges, top and bottom, were twisting snakes, and round the centre was a procession of almost life-sized jaguars, their mouths turned towards her in cruel, stylised snarls. She was hardly aware of him saying softly, *'El tigre*—the tiger—that's what the people here call him.'

> Tyger! Tyger! burning bright
> In the forests of the night ...

Without warning, the lines of Blake's poem leapt into Cal's mind; the frieze had the same menace, the unnerving vitality of primitive cave paintings—there was so much beauty yet so much savagery in this country. The snakes looked as though they were writhing off the walls towards her, and she almost heard the throaty half-purr, half-snarl as the great crimson-mouthed beasts crouched to spring at her.

Fear was stirring in her stomach, prickling the fine tawny-blonde hairs on her nape; she swallowed, took a step backwards and cannoned into Luis's arm, sending the torch skittering across the stone floor. When she swung round he was between her and the doorway, blotting out the light, and, thrown off balance, she flung her hands up against his chest to steady herself.

For one moment, wholly outside time, they stood frozen in the dim light, only their breath warm against each other's mouths, staring as though each were seeing the other for the first time. The hot blood was pulsing in Cal's brain, making it flash strange, unnerving messages to every part of her body. Luis's shadow, dark against the brilliance from the doorway, loomed over her, the utter blackness setting up faint echoes which vibrated softly all round her—within her—like a gently stroked bell.

She tore her hands away, blundering past him, and when a few moments later he followed her she was standing, her shallow, hurried breathing almost back to normal, staring out across the plaza. She moistened her lips.

'It—it was so claustrophobic in there. It must have been those paintings—all those snakes.' She forced a light laugh out of her tight throat.

'Yes, it must.' His voice was completely expressionless, and when she risked a furtive glance the only difference in his face was that it was a shade paler than usual.

'What a marvellous view.' A move to this topic was definitely safer, and, in any case, the whole of Cueltazan's ruined splendour lay beneath them. 'I wish I'd brought my camera up here.'

'I don't think you'd get much of an idea of perspective—wide shots like this are tricky.' There was only a cool detachment in his tone.

Beyond was the green land ocean, washing away in every direction and creeping insidiously towards them. In spite of the burning heat, she shivered.

'I get the feeling that the jungle's swallowed everything else and is just waiting for us to turn our backs.'

He shrugged. 'It was hidden for hundreds of

years.'

'But it mustn't be hidden again,' she burst out passionately. 'You mustn't let it.'

'You think so?' His voice had suddenly hardened. 'But maybe I have other priorities.'

Cal flushed under the implied rebuke, and she recalled what Father Aidan had told her of his plans for Chicambo—electricity, a school, help for children like Rosa, so desperate for work. And Chicambo wasn't even his responsibility—how many other villages, other Rosas was he intending to help?

'Yes, you're right,' she said in a low voice, not looking at him. 'People are far more important than any place, so—'

She broke off, surprised at herself. A few weeks ago, she would never have said that, much less thought it. What in the world was happening to her? She'd come out here to do her bit towards changing San Cristóbal, she thought wryly, and here was San Cristóbal subtly undermining all her most cherished views.

She paused for one last panoramic view, then said, 'Oh, there's another building over there. Can we have a look at it?'

He rolled his eyes in mock despair. 'I was hoping you wouldn't spot that. But never let it be said that any stone was left unturned to make your day complete. Come on, then.' He held out his hand. 'Catch hold and just look at the step below you, nothing else.'

She extended the very tips of her fingers towards his palm, but he gripped her hand tightly and together they took the first perilous step down the cliff-face.

Near the base of the pyramid was a single, huge block which formed a low table, and he gestured her to it. 'Wait here.'

She perched on the edge, watching him as he strode off towards the helicopter. Those long legs . . . the easy, animal-like grace of his walk . . . Cal, realising that her eyes were hungrily devouring him, angrily transferred all her attention to a couple of small lime-green lizards which were basking on the stone beside her . . .

'Maybe I should just have mentioned,' he was standing over her, lightly swinging a machete so that the sunlight winked off its wicked blade, 'there's an old superstition here—women come and sit on that stone to make sure that they have an—abundant family.'

As she leapt to her feet, she heard a soft chuckle. 'I shouldn't worry, *querida*. After all, surely it's more down to the lady's husband than a chunk of inanimate stone, don't you agree?'

'Oh, I should think so,' she said offhandedly, forcing herself to return his bland gaze.

He glanced down at her feet. 'Tuck your trousers into your boots.'

She opened her mouth to protest that it was far too hot, met his eyes, then sat down again, not on the stone, but on a hunk of grass.

As she struggled with her boots, he remarked, 'You obviously haven't been bitten by chiggers yet.'

She wrinkled her forehead. 'Chiggers? No, I don't think so. Mosquitoes, millions of them—and flies, but——'

'In that case, you haven't,' he said drily, 'because, believe me, you'd most certainly know if you had been. They're vicious little mites which live in thick undergrowth. If they get on you, they bore into the skin and set up a body reaction which nearly drives you crazy to scratch and usually ends up septic.'

'Ugh, horrible.' She glanced down at her bare arm, as though half expecting to see a swarm of voracious insects homing in on it. 'But I've got plenty of insect repellent on.'

He looked wholly unimpressed. 'I'm afraid chiggers regard all repellents as a tasty hors d'oeuvre before the main dish. But anyway, just watch out where you walk.'

He took up the machete and stood frowning, obviously trying to get his bearings. 'This way, I think.'

The jungle met them like a green wall, but at one point the faintest remnant of a path was just visible. Luis plunged in and began hacking methodically at the tangle of bamboo and creepers, Cal following in his wake, easing herself gingerly past the roughly hacked branches.

When he eventually paused for breath he wiped the back of his arm across his brow. He plunged the machete upright into the ground, then peeled off his shirt, across which damp patches of sweat had spread, and tied it round his waist. As he turned back to work, she saw little runnels of sweat trickling down his gleaming silky skin, the muscles rippling under it.

'Shall I take over for a bit?' she proffered diffidently.

'What? No, thanks. I wouldn't altogether trust you with this.' He spun the blade between his fingers so that a ray of sunlight filtering through the dense branches flashed on it. 'I'd hate to have my head lopped clean off my shoulders—even if it was accidental.'

Cal's lips tightened. 'I'm perfectly capable of chopping down a few bamboos,' she said tartly, and held out her hand. 'Please give it to me.'

He shrugged. 'OK.'

She took the machete and, pushing past him, began slashing at the wiry branches. His rhythmic, swinging movement had made it look so easy, but in her slippery hands the tool became a living creature with a will all its own. She gritted her teeth and struggled on grimly, hacking at every stem with an unrestrained ferocity, but then heard him say, 'Here, let me show you.'

At the same moment his arms went round her and his hands closed on hers. 'Just use your wrists, not your whole body. Look, like this.'

His deeply tanned hands tensed, forcing hers to take up his rhythm as he swung the blade from side to side. Together, they had sliced through several clumps of bamboo when he said, 'Got it now?'

'Think so.' It was all she could trust herself to say, held as she was in the circle of his arms, her senses almost overwhelmed by his nearness, his glowing skin, the hard tautness of his stomach and flanks, the warm, male scent of his body. When he moved back, abruptly releasing her, his touch, his skin brushing hers, the feel of his body pressed against hers, all of them still lingered so that her whole body felt filled with him.

He was still just behind her. Without daring to look at him, she gripped the blade and set to work, but after a few minutes, half blinded by sweat, she was forced to a breathless standstill.

'OK, point taken. You're a rough, tough woodsperson.' There was an undercurrent of lazy amusement in his voice, but when she glanced back at him she saw in his eyes something else—a gleam of respect?

He took the machete out of her sticky hands and set to work again. A few more strokes, then daylight was brilliant on their faces and ahead was a small clearing, roughly paved and sloping to a wide, fast-flowing stream.

On the nearer bank was the stone building Cal had spotted from the pyramid, long and low, with just one arched doorway and a couple of window holes. When she looked inside the air was dank and fetid, and from the shadows at the far end came little furtive rustlings. Bats? Scorpions? Probably only another harmless lizard, but all the same she retreated hastily.

Luis had dropped down by the stream and was splashing handfuls of water over his face and shoulders. The silver droplets gleamed on his black head and ran down his back as though he were some sleek-skinned animal.

She stood staring at him, transfixed by shafts of sheer pleasure-pain, until, sensing her behind him, he turned. A wholly new, infinitely disturbing expression flickered in his dark eyes for a moment, then they were as unrevealing as ever. He patted the bank.

'Come and cool off.'

She sat down beside him, but not too close, as he began taking off his boots.

'No leeches?' She gave him a sideways look from under her lashes and he shook his head.

'No, the current's too swift here.' He shot her a brief smile, but she turned away, quite unable to return it, and started to unlace her own boots.

The water was like cold silk and she leaned back on her hands, watching the eddies swirl around their two pairs of feet, hers pale-skinned and slender, his strong and deeply tanned. As they sat there, side by side, luxuriating in the coolness, she was suddenly filled with an almost overwhelming sense of isolation, of their utter aloneness, just the two of them together in this remote, barely accessible place.

Luis's voice broke into her thoughts. 'It opens into a pool just downstream. It's deep enough to swim there if you want.'

'Oh, no.' Strip to her underwear? 'I don't think I'll bother.'

'Please yourself. Take a look at it, though. It's man-made, and one theory is that this building housed sacrificial victims and they had their last ritual bathe there before being led off to the pyramid to be executed. Most of them were probably young virgins.' He paused. 'It clearly didn't pay to be a virgin in those days.'

'Does it ever?'

The words were out before she could hold them back and she bit her lip on the bitterness that, quite without warning, had welled up in her. 'Well, of course, darling,' Phil's voice clanged in her ear, 'if you hadn't been so hell-bent on hanging on to that bloody virginity of yours . . .'

Her hands clenched and she moved restlessly, then realised that another voice was saying softly, 'What's wrong, Cal?'

He was watching her closely, a look almost of concern in his eyes.

'Oh, nothing.' She shook herself free from the clinging ghosts of the past, forcing a self-deprecating smile. 'I was just thinking of those poor girls.'

Not meeting his eyes again, she scrambled up, dried her feet on a handful of grass, put her boots back on and went across to the building. She was working her way along one side, examining the closely interlocking masonry, when she caught sight of a large shrub covered with enormous pearly-white flower-buds, their reflexed petals drawn back over the tightly furled centres.

Luis had followed her and she looked up at him, her face flushed with excitement. 'It's a *Datura arborea*—it's got to be, but . . .'

With the very tip of one finger, she gently lifted one of the huge buds, but when he went to touch the plant she said sharply. 'Be careful. If I'm right, it's very poisonous—it's the nightshade family, angel's trumpet. And yet I'm almost sure there's no record of them ever being found in San

Cristóbal—in the wild, I mean.'

She bent forward and sniffed gingerly. 'Hmm, no scent yet, and I need to smell them to be sure. Angel's trumpets have a peculiar, musty smell, like nothing else, but the flowers won't open until evening, or at least late afternoon, so I shan't be certain till then.'

He shook his head. 'Sorry, honey, but we shan't be here then.'

'Why not?'

'Because I'm not hanging around, just waiting for the skies to open.'

'Rain, you mean?' She looked up at the cloudless sky. 'But it's not going to rain—it's the dry season, isn't it?'

He laughed derisively. 'There's no such thing as a dry season up here—it rains just as often as it feels like it. And besides, I've got a business appointment back at the hacienda this evening, which I don't intend breaking for—that.' He gestured dismissively towards the angel's trumpet.

'But you don't understand——'

'I understand perfectly well. Those flowers don't open till this evening—and we shan't be here this evening.'

'No, but——'

'But nothing. Sorry,' though there wasn't the faintest shred of regret in his voice, 'conversation closed.'

And with that he swung on his heel, picked up his machete and walked off down the path they had made, without even bothering to see if she was following him.

She watched him out of sight, her lips pursed. He was almost certainly right about the rain—after all, he did have a slightly longer acquaintance with the climate here than she had. But even so, need he have been quite so brutal, quite so—overbearing? No, of course not—but that was the man, wasn't it? On a scale of ten, he'd score twenty every time for arrogant disregard for every other living being.

But there was more than that, she acknowledged miserably to herself. What was wrong with them both, for heaven's sake? Rational, sensible people—and yet they couldn't be in one another's company for ten minutes without snarling at each other like a pair of angry jaguars on that frieze.

CHAPTER SEVEN

WHEN Cal at last returned to the plaza, a portable barbecue rack had been set up under the shade of a cotton tree and Luis was brushing oil over some enticingly fragrant kebabs and chicken portions.

'Hungry?'

He did not look up, but he sounded perfectly amiable. Well, he would, wouldn't he? she thought resentfully. He'd got his own way, which to someone like him was the *only* way, so it wouldn't even occur to him for a moment that her feathers might have been ruffled.

'Yes.'

She dropped the constrained monosyllable into the air between them, then sat down with her back against the tree.

'There's a rug on the rear seat. Sit on that—in case of ants,' he added, with a swift glance at her mutinous face, so she fetched it, along with her bag, which contained the picnic lunch she'd brought with her.

Rosa had made some small tortillas the previous evening and filled them with a spicy mixture of meat, red beans and tomatoes, which had smelled delicious at the time but which, after a night in the fridge and a morning in the broiling helicopter, now seemed rather less inviting. She was trying to summon up enough enthusiasm to take a bite when he stood over her, holding a plate piled high with kebabs and charcoal-grilled chicken.

'What the hell's that you've got?'

'My lunch,' she said coldly, and deliberately took a large bite of the limp, unappetising pancake. The next moment, he had banged down the plate, scooped the tortillas up off her lap and hurled them as far as he could towards the centre of the plaza.

She scowled up at him furiously. 'What d'you think you're playing at?'

'Giving the turkey vultures a feast. It might put a shine on their feathers—or maybe not.'

He squatted down on his haunches beside her and thrust the plate of meat on to her lap.

'When I offer to take a lady out for the day, I do not expect her to provide her own food.'

'I don't exactly remember you offering!' she snapped.

'Well, let's just say that I *have* brought you, shall we?' he retorted, then fished a serviette-wrapped knife and fork out of his shirt pocket and held them out to her. 'Now, get stuck in while I fetch the rest.'

He came back carrying a box from which he took several plastic containers holding a rice salad, green salad with its own portion of French dressing, a pale green avocado dip, bread rolls and butter.

'Help yourself.'

As she reluctantly obeyed, he sat beside her, ladled food on to his plate, then, with a glance at hers, piled more on to that.

She was halfway through her second kebab

when he asked, 'You approve of my cuisine?'

'Yes,' she admitted, 'these kebabs are really delicious.'

'I told you they were—roasted.'

She stopped chewing and gaped at him in slowly dawning horror.

'You mean——' she began, in a strangled voice.

He nodded, solemn-faced. 'Of course—iguana kebabs.' But his voice trembled on the last word, and he added confidingly, 'You know, that's the first time I've ever seen freckles turn green.' And the laughter burst out of him.

'Oh, you, you——' She caught his eye, her lips twitched, and she too erupted into laughter.

'Now, get on with it, before it gets cold.'

He gestured with his fork towards her plate and, all her resentment evaporated by that healing laugh, she went on eating. He really ought to laugh more often, she thought—his smiles were rare enough, but in that one instant the harshly etched lines of strain round his eyes and mouth had all but vanished, and the pain which always seemed to hover behind his eyes melted.

'Wine?'

'Oh, yes, please.'

From the chill box he brought out a bottle of sparkling white wine, opened it and handed her a glass, smoking white in the heat.

'Mmm, lovely.' She smiled at him. 'We may be a thousand miles from civilisation, but you certainly know how to barbecue in style.'

'Yes, I suppose I learnt that particular art in the States.'

'You must have spent a lot of time up there,' she said with studied casualness.

'Is that a statement or a question?'

There was an immediate wariness, a drawing back, but she persisted. 'Both, I suppose.'

He eyed her levelly for a moment, then shrugged. 'Well, I trained as an attorney at Harvard, I practised in New York, but then——' a fractional hesitation '—I came back last year, when my father died and I took over the Palomita estates.'

She sensed that there was more—much more—behind the spare words. 'Why didn't you come back earlier?'

'There were—to coin a phrase—reasons.'

Her exact words to him—she realised that, like her, he'd pulled down that invisible 'No Trespassing' shutter between them and no amount of probing would get any more from him.

She took a sip of the dry white wine. 'Palomita. That means little dove, doesn't it?'

He nodded.

'But I haven't seen any doves in the forest.'

'No, it was my grandfather's pet name for my grandmother. Until then, it was the Hacienda Revilla. They were married when he was twenty-five and she was seventeen.'

'Oh, how romantic,' Cal murmured dreamily.

'You think so?'

'And I suppose they lived happily ever after.'

'Not really.' His tone was empty of expression. 'She died at eighteen, when my father was born. My grandfather lived till he was eighty, but he never married again.'

'The poor man.' In her imagination, Cal saw an older Luis, lonely and embittered, perpetually riding the forest trails of the estate, of which the very name must have been a daily, anguished reminder of the young girl he'd lost. 'And yet, if he loved her so much, maybe he thought that even fifty years of sadness was worth it.'

He gave a bitter laugh. 'What a sentimental little fool you are. But perhaps you've not yet learned the price the gods demand for love.'

She glanced at him sharply. There was surely more—a great deal more behind his words than his grandfather's tragic story, but she was beginning to know him well enough to realise that to press him further would be futile.

'Maybe not,' she said at last, in a low voice, 'although I've known something of it.'

'Tell me, Cal.' His words were gentle now, and he took her hand, softly brushing his thumb across the back, so that under its almost hypnotic influence she went on.

'There's nothing to tell, really. I was engaged, and Phil, my fiancé, he—found somebody else. I called at his flat unexpectedly and found him in bed with her.' She pulled a rueful face. 'But I suppose that sort of thing happens all the time.'

He squeezed her hand gently. 'But the pain is none the less, *querida*.'

After a moment, he loosed his hold and she sat enmeshed in her own thoughts, barely aware that he had reached into the chill box and brought out a pineapple. Deftly, he removed the top, cut it into thin slices, and she began to eat mechanically.

'And what's going on behind those beautiful topaz eyes, I wonder?'

She started. 'Beautiful?' she repeated stupidly.

'Of course. But surely you realise that?' he said matter-of-factly, as the warm colour swept into her cheeks. 'Beautiful eyes, beautiful face—at least, it would be if you didn't insist on cutting your lovely hair with a pair of garden shears.'

He smiled, but she did not respond. Beautiful? He really thought she was beautiful? She was still struggling to retrieve her composure when he went on, 'But tell me, what were you thinking?'

'Oh, nothing.' Cal forced a careless smile, but she could feel the threads tightening round her even more and she was filled with a desperate need to distance herself from this handsome, enigmatic man. She snatched at a topic which, she hoped, would do just that. 'Well, if you must know, I was wondering, now that you've taken over the estate, what plans you have for the forest.'

He gave her a long, level look and topped up his wine glass.

'Since you ask, I'm intending to cut down part of it.'

She opened her mouth, but then shut it again as he went on, 'A lot of the trees, particularly the mahogany, have reached full maturity and I'm going to clear them. With the proceeds I'm setting up a sawmill so that in future the timber can be planked and finished here, which will generate more jobs and ensure much better money for the people. For one thing, I hope it'll stop the drift of young kids to the towns, where they straight away get lured into drugs or prostitution.' He eyed her sardonically. 'I trust you have no objections?'

'No, of course not. That's marvellous.'

'Hmm.' That cool, appraising look again. 'But surely it suits you and your little friends to think every landowner is a greedy, grasping robber baron?'

'Not at all,' she said defensively, 'we're not that naïve. We just want to see the land properly managed.' Her eyes strayed to the pyramid and its crumbling façade. 'But in the meantime this place could just rot slowly away, and that would be terrible. If you could persuade people to invest money here—not to spoil it, but to encourage tourism. A road, an overnight hotel . . .'

Swept on by her own eloquence, she was already seeing the low white building, set unobtrusively among the trees. 'I know in one way it would destroy the magic of this place, but the development could be tightly controlled. You'd have to involve the Tourist Board, of course, the government——'

'How many more times do I have to tell you,' he cut in savagely, 'not to try to run my life for me? If I'd known you were going to start on that tack again, I'd never have brought you within a million miles of this place.'

'All right, I'm sorry.' She hastily backed off from yet another confrontation. 'It's none of my business.'

'Too right, it's not.' His breathing had steadied again and he drained his wine glass, then began to gather the dishes together.

'Oh, let me do that. I'd be glad to.'

So he settled himself comfortably back against the tree, arms folded, his sun-hat tilted forward. From the shadow of its brim, though, she could feel his eyes on her as, rather self-consciously, she packed away, but by the time she had finished they were closed.

She had unobtrusively picked up her bag and was tiptoeing away when he said, 'And just where are you pussyfooting off to?'

'I'm going to do some sketching.'

He groaned. 'Are you hyperactive or something? Don't you ever rest?'

'Yes, but I don't want to waste a second of my time here. After all,' and she felt a sudden twist of pain at the thought, 'I'll never see this place again.'

'Never's a long time, *querida*.' He spread his hands expressively. 'You never know, in twenty years' time I might even have taken your advice and built a six-lane freeway, an airport and half a dozen multi-storey hotels. And what would you think of that, I wonder? But anyway, if you want to kill yourself in this heat, go right ahead. Just don't do a disappearing act. Don't forget—we're leaving soon.'

'I haven't forgotten,' was all that she allowed herself to say.

He pulled his hat down over his eyes again, so she favoured him with one brief scowl then picked up her bag and walked off. The afternoon heat was too much for her to venture for long into the open expanse of the plaza, so instead she moved gratefully from one tree to another, taking photographs and making quick sketches as she went.

Her circular route brought her near to the path they had made earlier. The first angel's trumpet flowers might be starting to open—she glanced at her watch, then up at the sky, still perfectly blue except for the faintest wisps of white cloud, like gauzy lace on the shoulders of the mountains. Finally, she sneaked an oblique look across to the far side of the square, but Luis lay exactly where she'd left him—he hadn't moved a muscle. Just ten minutes, that was all it would take . . .

She looked eagerly at the huge cream buds, but they were still tightly furled. She tapped her foot with vexation and was turning away when she noticed, with a flicker of excitement, that one of the very topmost buds was opening. She reached up her nose towards it and caught a slight whiff of its musty odour, then stood frowning at it, willing it to open fully.

She fetched out her camera and tried to select the best angle, looking slightly upwards, with other buds behind it. She took one shot, but it would be even better—ideal perhaps for the cover of next year's PET calendar—if the wretched thing would co-operate instead of just sitting there fighting a silent battle of wills with her.

Just a few more minutes, surely? What was Luis doing? Still sleeping the sleep of the just, she hoped. Even so, the thought of his face if he did find her here made her quake with terror. But if he did wake, it would take him some time to search her out and drag her back to the helicopter—and she could well have got the perfect shot by then.

She eased her T-shirt away from her neck. Her skin felt uncomfortably hot, so that it smarted and tingled; her eyes wandered past the shrub to the pool, its limpid water cool and so inviting ... There was no sound, no angry footsteps.

Terrified at her own daring, she kicked off her boots and socks, tore off her clothes—she'd left off her bra for coolness—and slid down off the bank. The water came to her shoulders and she walked out a few paces to stand, groaning quietly to herself with sensuous pleasure. Near the surface, the water had been warmed by the sun, but lower down, past her thighs, it still had something of the delicious chill from where it had risen in springs in the mountains.

It was true what Luis had said—she was in a giant stone basin and she could feel the artificial smoothness under her feet. What had those young girls thought as they'd stood here? Perhaps they'd believed that they were going to be married to the god, and then, at the top of the pyramid, the gleaming obsidian knife had come down ...

When Luis had told her the story, tossing the word virgin out with casual cruelty, he couldn't have realised the sharp inner anguish he would rouse in her ... 'Of course, darling, if only you'd been a bit more forthcoming ...' Phil's final, brutal phone call surged back, bringing something of its original pain with it. She'd asked herself often enough why she'd clung so obstinately—as he saw it—to her refusal to sleep with him once they were engaged. Now, she knew that it was simply because she had never really loved him.

But at least Phil had lost forever the power to hurt her. Luis Revilla, though . . . What had he said? She was beautiful? She looked down and saw her body, white and faintly unreal through the greenish water. She smiled down at that stranger's body and, hardly aware of what she was doing, spread her arms in a voluptuous little gesture.

Was she really beautiful? Oh, for heaven's sake, she thought scornfully, don't be so simple! He speaks such perfect, easy English that you forget, but he isn't a westerner, is he? He's a Latin-American, and they're born with charm oozing out of their fingertips—he probably learned pretty little speeches like that in the schoolroom, and the delicate art of seduction in the nursery.

On the other hand, if she didn't get back up that path very soon it wouldn't be any pretty speeches she'd be hearing. She heaved herself out, mopped herself on a handful of tissues, then pulled on her clothes. Mmm, marvellous—cool and refreshed from head to toe, and with any luck that hard-to-get flower would be open by now.

She tugged her bag up on to her shoulder, turned, then stood, quite motionless. She'd dressed under the shade of a tree, and as she'd swung round she'd caught fleetingly, out of the very corner of her eye, a slight, almost furtive movement.

Without turning her head, she lifted her eyes and saw, with a sickening plunge of her stomach, that along one of the lower branches lay a snake. It was at least six feet long and turquoise-green, almost the same colour as the leaves, and she wouldn't have seen it if it hadn't still been slightly moving, its head resting against the leafy branch.

As she stared, the narrow, pointed head was raised slightly and the reptile gazed at her unblinkingly, its forked tongue flicking lazily to and fro. It was between her and the path, and the pool was behind her. If she edged sideways—but all the muscles in her legs had turned to water and they would not obey the message that her brain was shrieking at them. All that she could register was that that head had suddenly lifted and tensed——

'Don't move!' Then, as she started, even more sharply, 'Keep still!'

But then a cry was wrenched from her as Luis leaped forward, gave her a violent shove which sent her staggering sideways and, simultaneously, swung a large branch at the snake's head. There was an angry hiss, a sinuous, rustling movement, and the creature had gone. Luis followed it to the undergrowth, then came back to where she was standing, her eyes still hugely dilated with the terror she had felt. She longed for the release of tears, but could only stare at him, dry-eyed.

'What the hell d'you think you were playing at? You disobedient little——' He bit off the word. 'I told you not to wander off.' His face was contorted with fury; his cheeks, which a moment before had been deathly pale, were flushed dark red. 'Will you ever learn to do as you're told?'

He seized hold of her and shook her fiercely, then just as abruptly let go his hold, so that she backed up against the tree trunk to save herself from falling.

'I-I'm sorry,' she whispered through ashen lips. 'W-was it poisonous?'

'Of course it bloody was! Just think yourself lucky it was a parrot snake and not a fer de lance—it would have come straight for you and you'd have been vulture fodder by now, you stupid, stupid little bitch!'

'No—please.' She flinched from his fury. Her whole body was shuddering violently with reaction; her head felt as though it were going to shake right off its stalk.

She put her hand to her face, biting the palm to stop the huge sob which was burning its way up through her. But it burst out, and the next moment he was pulling her roughly into his arms.

'Oh, *querida*, don't look like that—please don't.' His voice was ragged, and he held her, one arm round her, the other pressing her head tightly to his chest. His cheek was against her hair and he made soothing, incoherent noises into it, until the terrible paroxysm of shaking at last eased to a faint quiver.

He held her away from him and gazed down at her, sombre-eyed, then very gently, with his little finger, lifted the two unshed tears that glinted on the ends of her lashes and blew them softly away.

'All right now?'

She nodded, unable to trust her voice.

'Oh, God, what you do to me.' He gave her a

shaky smile. 'If every hair on my head hasn't turned grey soon because of you——'

His lips tightened and they stared at one another from one heartbeat to the next, then he dragged her to him again, his mouth closing over hers, hard and demanding. He thrust his tongue between her lips, probing for the moist softness within, then slid his hand to the back of her head, his fingers tangling in her thick hair, and pressed her mouth to his until she felt his teeth cut through the tender flesh.

But the pain went almost unnoticed as, deep within her, passion flickered then flared into avid life to meet his. Her hands had been trapped between their chests, their two hearts clamouring against them; she dragged them free and slid them round behind his back, gripping handfuls of shirt and flesh to strain him to her.

He raised his head briefly to look at her, a long, searching look, and she saw the hunger, dark and insatiable, blazing in his eyes. When he slid one hand up inside her damp T-shirt the touch of each finger was like small electric shocks racing across her smooth skin, and when it fastened on the firm swell of her breast the faint sigh he gave was muffled against her hair.

She sagged against him, the bones in her legs, like the rest of her body, melting like wax from the fierce body heat which emanated from him. He braced himself against her to balance them both, then, with what seemed endless slowness, they sank to their knees, holding on to each other, straining together as though they were already one flesh . . .

The huge drops of icy rain fell on their faces almost unnoticed—it was the first crash of thunder that jerked them back to reality. With a smothered curse, Luis, his eyes still dazed with passion, drew back and looked up at the sky.

The next moment he had whiplashed to his feet and was pulling her up beside him. Holding on to her wrist, he snatched up her bag, which lay abandoned beside them, and began dragging her towards the track. Cal could hear those enormous raindrops pattering spasmodically all round them, but otherwise everything—birds, insects, even the faint breeze in the canopy of leaves—had gone silent, as though intently waiting.

They had almost reached the helicopter when the rain really started—exactly as if someone had emptied a sky-sized bucket of water over them. Luis pushed her in, then threw himself in alongside her and slid the door to. The helicopter was rocking under the force of the deluge, and hailstones beat incessantly against it in a deafening staccato.

Cal felt her hands clenching convulsively. She'd experienced plenty of tropical downpours in the past few weeks, but this one was something special. The cannonades of thunder, lightning flickering endlessly across the plaza, the roar of the rain—it was like being trapped under a gigantic waterfall—dazing, mind-blowing.

'How long will it last, do you think?' She had to shout above the tumult.

He shrugged unamiably. 'God knows. All night

if it feels like it.'

'All night?' She stared at him aghast. 'But you've got an appointment.'

'Yes, I have, haven't I?'

Cal hung her head miserably, the wet strands of hair dripping against her neck. 'I'm sorry, really I am.'

He gave a mirthless laugh. 'Sorry—for what? Merely for making me miss my appointment—or for doing your damnedest to stand my whole life on its head?'

He gave her one withering look, then deliberately turned his head away. But Cal, staring straight ahead through the rain-crazed windscreen, sensed that not all his anger was directed against her. He was furious with himself, so furious that he could barely trust himself to speak, and it could only be because of that moment of madness by the pool. If the storm hadn't broken, what folly might he—might they—have committed? And it *was* folly, she told herself fiercely. However attracted she might be to him, she knew for certain that any entanglement with him could only lead to heartbreak on a scale which she could not even begin to imagine . . .

Darkness had fallen before the storm abated and the rain eased to a drizzle. The silence in the cabin had lasted a very long time, and Cal cleared her throat.

'Can't we leave now?'

He jabbed an impatient thumb in the direction of the pyramid and, peering out, she could just make out the low clouds swathing its summit.

'But surely you can take off? You've got instruments.'

'Flying blind in ten-metre visibility? You may fancy being smashed against the nearest mountainside, but I don't.'

He knelt up and began clearing the rear seat.

'What are you doing?'

'I don't suppose you want to sleep with the barbecue in the small of your back.' He glanced briefly at her face. 'Where else did you plan on spending the night?'

She clutched briefly at the possibility of bedding down alone in one of the ruined buildings, but the thought of almost certainly finding herself with a scorpion or a snake as a bedfellow made the hairs on her neck lift. Not, of course, that he was any less lethal than anything that might be waiting outside . . .

She grabbed her bag and scrambled inelegantly over the seat. Her wet clothes were still clinging to her, and in the sudden chill after the storm her teeth were beginning to chatter softly.

'Get out of those wet things.' She heard him fumbling under the front seat, and a moment later the chunky sweater he'd been wearing that morning landed beside her. 'Put this on.'

'What about you?' she protested, but he only repeated his command harshly. She still hesitated, but he had subsided into his seat, staring straight ahead—whatever chemistry had briefly ignited between them was now utterly dead. She wriggled out of her clothes, pulled the soft warmth of the sweater over her head and wrapped herself in the rug.

Beside her were the flying jackets. 'Here, have this.' She thrust one over the divide and he took it with a grunt, peeled off his shirt and put it on.

Cal curled up and closed her eyes. At first, she was far too aware of her surroundings to relax, her nerve-ends twitching at his nearness, but gradually the light pattering of rain made a soothing pattern in her brain, and she slept . . .

She was in the forest. She was alone. It was night, but all around her were furtive rustlings as a million creatures watched her. Just ahead, someone was making a pathway—she could hear them slashing at the undergrowth, see a bright blade gleaming. But she couldn't see who it was and, terrified of being left alone, she was stumbling along behind.

And then she stepped on something soft, something that moved under her, that reared up in front of her, then coiled itself in smothering folds around her body——

'Wake up, Cal.'

A hand was on her arm and, with a last gasp of sick horror, she tore herself free of the dream and lay sweating, her heart leaping in her chest. She opened her eyes and saw, out of the blackness, a face bending towards her.

'Luis?' she said shakily. 'I-I was having a nightmare.' She shuddered convulsively, feeling the remnants of those serpent coils still loosely twined around her. 'Did I cry out, or something?'

There was a soft chuckle in the darkness. 'You

could say that.'

'Oh, I'm sorry. It was stupid of me.'

'Don't apologise for nightmares, Cal—anyone can have them. I've certainly had my share.' There was a *frisson* of something in his voice, but then it was gone. 'Now, move over.'

And then he was across the divide, dropping into the seat beside her. He took hold of her hand. 'You're shivering.'

Picking up the rug, which had fallen to the floor, he wrapped her in it, then half lifted her so that she was lying curled against him, his arms round her. There was not the remotest sexual threat in his embrace now, just gentle reassurance, and with a sigh she snuggled up to him.

'Now, go back to sleep.'

'But you——' she protested sleepily.

'It's almost morning. I shan't sleep again.'

He cradled her head to him, and began stroking her hair, a gentle, rhythmic movement. She yawned, and her eyes closed.

CHAPTER EIGHT

ANA GUTIERREZ finished her speech of glowing introduction and thrust the microphone at Cal. Looking out at the mass of expectant faces and waving PET banners, stretching away across the sun-baked lawns of the university campus, she somehow fought down the cowardly impulse to shove the microphone at someone else, and instead tried to moisten her lips with the tip of her dry tongue.

What on earth had possessed her? she asked herself yet again, then thought grimly, Lunacy, sheet lunacy, that was what it was. At the time, it had seemed such a good idea to spend a long weekend sightseeing in Santa Clara—after all, she'd seen nothing of the capital and she was leaving San Cristóbal in less than two weeks. Her work was all but finished, and Pete, fully recovered now, would soon be back in charge.

And then, to drop in on the rally being held by the local students' PET group, to protest against plans to build a tourist complex right on the beach where, for millions of years, sea-turtles had come to lay their eggs—well, that had been a marvellous bonus.

But now the entire carefully planned weekend was falling apart at the seams. A terrible ride on that rattletrap bus, with that foul-breathed billy goat on the seat behind snorting down her neck for the entire seven-hour journey . . . that appallingly sleazy hotel, with its leering desk clerk, where she hadn't been able to sleep a wink all night because of the incessant comings and goings . . . and now she'd been inveigled into speaking at the rally.

Ana, the local PET group leader, gave her a wink of encouragement and pushed her forward, to a burst of enthusiastic applause, and Cal began speaking, very hesitantly at first, in a mixture of English and Spanish, but then more confidently as the thoughts began to flow.

It was all very simple, really, she declared—she'd been involved in a very similar campaign that they'd won in Southern Europe. No one was denying the need for tourism, but the authorities had to be persuaded to move the complex half a mile down the coast to another, equally attractive beach. The only problem was the owner of the beach, who was refusing point-blank to sell—or, rather, was demanding an impossibly high price. All the government had to do was give him a fair price, and put a compulsory sequestration order on the land.

Spurred on by the rapturous applause, Cal was rapidly forgetting her self-imposed caution, and she launched into a scathing attack on all the private, money-crazed landowners of San Cristóbal.

'Take the rain forests, for example, where a handful of owners are sitting on thousands upon thousands of hectares of land. Do you realise that the forests, worldwide, are home to over fifty per cent of our plant and animal species, and they're disappearing at a rate, every single day, of forty hectares a minute?'

The cheers were going to her head like strong wine and she hurtled on. 'And then there are those faceless, stateless, profit-mad multinational companies that are buying up the forests and ruthlessly exploiting . . .'

Her eyes swept across the ranks of waving banners, then all at once she faltered and ground to a halt, staring in horrified disbelief. Oh, no, it couldn't be. Her eyes flickered away, then back, but the mirage was still there and becoming more concrete every second. But what on earth was *he* doing here? Father Aidan had told her he was out of the country on a business trip, hadn't he? And yet, here he was, unmistakable, head and shoulders above those around him at the back of the crowd, standing apparently transfixed by her words.

He was frowning—no, scowling ferociously. Even at this distance she could feel the fierce anger breaking over her like a wave and, for a terrifying moment, she really thought he was going to thrust his way through the mass of students and drag her off the platform.

She struggled to recover herself, pretending that her command of Spanish had temporarily let her down, then thought, Oh, don't be a fool—he can't do anything to you, not here. But the thread of her speech had been broken, and she wound up rapidly then handed the microphone back to Ana.

Two young men with guitars struck up a rousing

song which everyone knew except Cal, so she edged to the rear of the platform and sat down. She shot a furtive glance at where Luis had been standing, then let out a sigh of relief—he'd gone. Whatever appalling coincidence had brought him to the campus, he would obviously be no more inclined to meet up with her than she with him.

After all, she hadn't set eyes on him for weeks—not since that early morning when they'd arrived back from Cueltazan. She'd woken at first light, feeling vaguely bereft, then had realised that he was no longer beside her. He'd been back in the front seat, clearly impatient to leave. He'd been moody and withdrawn during the totally silent flight, and when she'd refused his perfunctory invitation to breakfast his relief had been obvious. Deliberately obvious, she'd amended, as though to show her that that day of companionship, albeit uneasy, and more, that moment of passion by the pool, the tender concern after her nightmare, had both been aberrations that he had no intention of repeating . . .

Phew, it was hot—even hotter down here near the coast. And the rally was rapidly developing into a noisy foretaste of the fund-raising rock concert Ana had persuaded her to attend that evening. She fanned herself ineffectually with her sun-hat—she'd have to get into the shade soon or she would pass out.

Surely, just round the corner, screened by those hibiscus bushes, she remembered seeing a bench. Screened by the singing, wildly gyrating figures, she climbed down from the platform, crept across the grass and sank down gratefully on the shaded seat. The singing and cheers had faded slightly and she sat back, her eyes closed, so that she sensed rather than saw the figure that loomed up over her.

She leaped to her feet and went to run, but too late. With the speed of a jungle cat he'd pounced and was holding her arm in a vice-like grip.

'Not so fast, my little rabble-rouser. I want a word with you—or rather,' he amended grimly, 'quite a few words.'

Reluctantly, she turned to face him. He was wearing a beautifully cut lightweight silver-grey suit, white shirt and steel-grey tie; the jacket was moulded to his powerful chest and shoulders, the trousers held his long legs in a tight embrace. Until now, she'd never seen him in other than very casual clothes, and the effect was devastating—at once more polished and even more lethal.

He swung her round and began to drag her in the opposite direction, away from the sanctuary of the rally, his fingers biting deep into the soft flesh of her forearm.

'Let me go, will you?' She was panting with the effort to keep up with his determined strides. 'You're hurting me.'

'Good,' was the only reply, and when she tried to wrench herself free he brought her up short with an angry jerk, forcing her arm down so that she was close enough to him to receive the full menace of his anger.

'Get it into your head—willing or unwilling, you're coming with me. Now, walk.'

He steered her across the car park to where a bright red Ferrari Testarossa was parked in the shade of a jacaranda tree, and flung open the nearside door.

'Get in.'

'No, I won't,' she hurled at him defiantly. 'Apart from the fact that I'll do as I damn well please—ouch,' as his fingers tightened painfully, 'if you think I'm ever going to get into a gas-guzzler like that . . .' She scowled at the car. 'If anyone here saw me, I'd never lift my head for shame again.'

He opened the door wider. 'In.' When she still drew back, he went on threateningly, 'Are you going to get in, or do I have to pick you up and dump you in? Make up your mind, but I'm not staying round here any longer—some of your little friends might just come along and decide that all they need to make their day complete, after that inspiring speech of yours, is to string up a wicked landowner from the nearest tree.'

He gave her a shove, which tumbled her into the car, then slammed the door and stood glaring down at her, breathing hard. 'God, I could strangle you sometimes, do you know that?'

Then, before she could even toy with the idea of leaping out, he was in the seat beside her and firing the ignition. He backed out of the parking space at a speed which made her blench and accelerated down the winding drive, the huge, sleek car responding instantly to his barely controlled fury.

Once out on the main road to town, though, the weekend traffic forced him to slow and they cruised along, Luis tapping the fingers of his left hand in an impatient tattoo on the window-frame.

'What the hell are you doing in Santa Clara, anyway? I thought this was one place I could come without fear of meeting up with you.' They'd been silent for so long that she jumped when he spoke.

'I might ask the same of you,' she replied coldly, not deigning to turn her head.

'I had business down here. Did you?'

'In a way, yes.'

'Oh, yes, of course, I saw you.'

'And what brought *you* to the university? Spying on us, I suppose.' Oh, God, here they were again—fighting, snarling at each other like a pair of those painted jaguars.

'I'd been visiting a friend of mine—he's the head of the law faculty here. I hadn't realised I was going to be treated to such a scintillating demonstration of mob oratory, though.'

'If you must know, if I'd guessed they were going to get me to speak, I wouldn't have gone.'

But he laughed harshly. 'And pass up the chance to lambaste me? Don't give me that.'

'Look, I wasn't getting at you, honestly. In fact——' she raised her voice over his snort of disbelief '—I was going on to talk about the few enlightened landlords. But then, when I saw you—well, you put me off,' she added ingenuously.

But he only said coldly, 'I wonder why? Could it perhaps have been a guilty conscience?'

'No, it wasn't,' she yelled at him in total frustration, then turned her head, her lips in a tight line, to stare out of the window.

She saw a narrow road she recognised. 'You can put me down here,' she said icily. 'My hotel's just along there.'

He flashed her one surprised glance, then braked abruptly and, oblivious of the blaring horns, swung down the road.

'Put me down here,' she repeated obstinately.

'Don't be a fool. I'm not letting you walk here on your own.'

'Oh, not the big macho act again, please.' She gave a mock groan. 'For your information, I walked all round here yesterday evening and again this morning, and I'm still in one piece.'

'Don't push your luck, then——'

'There's the hotel. Thanks for the lift.'

But when she put her hand on the door-catch he leaned across and snapped it to.

'Who told you to stay *here*, for God's sake?'

Well, the Hotel Esmeralda did look rather run down and could certainly do with a good coat of paint, but need he be quite so insensitive?

'I asked at the bus station when I arrived.' Those marvellous sooty eyes were very close to hers, and all of a sudden she was finding it difficult to breathe. 'My—my guidebook says, always ask a local.'

'Well, you picked the wrong local, sweetie.'

There was more than a spark of laughter in his eyes now, but at least it enabled her to break free of the spell. 'Why—because it's cheap? We can't all afford to stay at the Santa Clara Astoria, you know—or perhaps you don't.'

'This place may call itself a hotel, but somehow

I don't think the fact that it's been closed down five times in the past year by the vice squad has anything to do with any deficiencies in its hotel business.'

'You mean——' Her eyes had widened in shocked incredulity.

He nodded. 'Yes. It doubles as a *casa de putas*.' Then, impatiently, when she frowned at him, 'A whore-house.'

Cal's jaw sagged and she let out her breath in a long, horror-stricken 'Oh.'

He got out and opened her door. 'Come on.'

'But——'

'You want to collect your things, don't you? Well, I'm coming with you. I presume you escaped—er—unscathed last night, but you might not be so lucky again.'

That same hateful desk clerk was lounging behind the plastic flowers. He eyed them knowingly but then, when Luis favoured him with one searing glance and a few curt words, he hastily fished out her room key.

Upstairs, she was forced to pack her rucksack and bag under Luis's watchful gaze, having to brush past him as he stood in the middle of the small room, as if even to perch on the rickety chair might somehow soil him. She worked in grim silence, furious with herself, and furious with him for having witnessed her shame. Back downstairs, he threw the key and a pile of banknotes down on to the desk and they went out, the clerk's lascivious eyes boring into her spine.

He handed her back into the car, then, as he

glanced over his shoulder to ease it out into the flow of traffic, said in that superior tone which so set her teeth on edge, 'You really aren't safe to be let out alone. God knows what would have happened to you, if I——'

'Well, nothing did happen, did it?' Infuriated, she swung round on him. 'If it comes to that, how come you know that place? Maybe you're one of their most favoured clients.'

He jammed on the brakes, so that she almost hurtled through the windscreen. 'Never say that again—do you hear?'

His voice was perfectly controlled, but the anger throbbed in it and, frightened of what her hasty words had unleashed, she said, 'Yes, I'm sorry. It's just that you make me so angry.'

'The feeling's entirely mutual, lady,' he said between his teeth, and, crashing the gears, he drove off.

'You're not going back to Chicambo, are you?' she asked in sudden alarm. 'I'm staying for the weekend.'

'So am I. No, I'm just taking you to somewhere slightly more salubrious than your last hotel.'

Beyond the suburbs at the far side of town, just where the road began to wind up towards the mountains, he turned off down a side-road, through an archway in a high white wall, and drew up on a gravelled drive. The building beyond was set among beautifully tended gardens and groves of huge palms, and through the open car window the scent of frangipani drifted in the airless afternoon heat.

Cal clenched the handle of her bag with perspiring fingers. 'But I can't stay here.' She bit her lip. 'I really can't.' But he was already lifting out her rucksack from the rear seat. 'Will you listen to me for once?' she said, her voice rising in desperation as he ushered her out. 'I won't go in there. I simply cannot afford it—and you certainly aren't paying for me.' As he shrugged, a sudden thought struck her. 'I'll ring Ana. She's already offered to——'

'Forget it. I'm not letting you out of my sight again until you're safely back in Chicambo. You're staying here—with me.'

The mixture of rage at him taking her over and terror at the thought of spending the night in close proximity to him fizzed up inside her like the head on a bottle of champagne.

'Once and for all, will you stop ordering me about? I'm not staying here. I'm going to ring Ana from reception, and then I'm leaving—leaving—leaving!'

She strode off down the path, her cheeks flaring with temper. She risked just one glance behind her and saw him meekly following her. Good, at last he's got the message, she thought savagely, and went on in through the open doorway. A smartly uniformed maid was just setting down a bowl of white gladioli on a polished table in the spacious hall.

'*Por favor, señorita,*' Cal began. '*Quiero telefonear*——' then stiffened as a hand closed over her elbow.

'Maria, please tell Señora Valdez that I have a

guest tonight.' Cal could just about follow the rapid Spanish and she suddenly went limp. 'Will she please prepare the guest suite, and ask her to serve tea in fifteen minutes. We'll have it in the garden.'

As Cal went to speak, his hand tightened warningly and she subsided, allowing herself to be led into a large room, shuttered against the blinding glare outside. He closed the door behind them, relinquished his hold and walked across to the nearest shutter.

As he opened it, she said, 'This is your house, isn't it?'

'That's right.'

Well, of course, a rich man like him wasn't going to be content with just one million-hectare hacienda, was he—he'd obviously need a fabulous town villa as well, wouldn't he? But, even so, need she have been quite so slow-witted?

'Sit down.' He gestured her to the elegant cream-brocaded sofa, and, after a split second, she dropped into it.

He took off his pale grey jacket and laid it on a chair, then unhooked his tie and tossed it down on to it, never taking his eyes off her for a moment. She felt a flicker of fear, then thought, Pull yourself together. He's only trying to dominate you, browbeat you, so just show the swine you don't go down that easily.

She jutted her chin and tried to look nonchalantly round the room, but it was very difficult to look unimpressed.

Every superb piece of furniture was obviously hand-picked, the wood—local mahogany, she

guessed—glowing with centuries of care. A large
cabinet stood in one corner, filled with delicate
English china figurines—Chelsea, Rockingham
and Worcester, the sort she'd only ever seen in
stately homes—and everywhere porcelain bowls of
flowers echoed the floral design in the old rose silk
Persian carpet.

She half turned her head to complete her survey
of the room, and saw on the wall behind her the
portrait of a dark-haired woman, young, beautiful,
vibrant with life.

'Who's that?' The words were out before she
remembered that she was refusing to show a grain
of interest in anything in this house.

'My wife—my former wife,' he amended, as she
swung round to face him, wide-eyed. His voice was
empty of emotion, and when she stared at him he
was engrossed in sorting through a pile of letters
on a desk.

Well, of course—she'd left him. No red-blooded
woman would be able to stand being married to
him for long.

He dropped the final envelope, straightened up
and came across to her, then stood regarding her,
his eyes narrowed slightly.

'Right now—let's get it straight, shall we? Once
and for all, get off my back.'

Stung, she could only counter with, 'And what
precisely do you mean by that?'

'Just this.' The cut-glass chandelier over their
heads tinkled in a sudden breeze, the sound
matching the ice in his voice. 'If I ever catch you
making speeches again about me, stirring up those

bloody interfering friends of yours——'

'But I've told you——'

'So help me, I'll get hold of you and give you such a thrashing that you won't be able to sit down until you're back in England—which is where you belong.'

She gave a gasp of outrage. 'How dare you? Just you try it, that's all.'

'Don't tempt me, honey, or I might just do that. You are an interfering, blabbering, self-righteous pest.'

Cal leapt to her feet. 'Well, let me tell you, of all the arrogant, overbearing——' She broke off, hunting desperately for insults, and her eyes fell on the portrait. Long past caution, she gestured fiercely towards it. 'It's no wonder she left you.'

'What do you mean?'

The ice had become glacial, but she swept on, 'No woman could bear to live with you—you're just totally impossible.'

'My wife is dead.'

The stark words reverberated in the sudden silence, and she was still staring at him, her mouth open, when there was a knock, the door opened and a grey-haired woman in black appeared.

'Shall I serve tea now, Señor Revilla?'

'Yes, thank you, Señora Valdez,' he replied, though his eyes were still locked with Cal's. 'We'll have it in the garden.'

Abruptly, he broke the lock, turning on his heel, and Cal followed him out to a courtyard, which was enclosed on three sides by the wings of the house, and open on the fourth to a belt of trees, beyond which were the mountains, blue-hazed in the heat.

In the centre was a circular stone basin, with a fountain playing over a mossy stone cherub holding a water jar, and with big pottery tubs of petunias and geraniums grouped round it. In the shade of some bamboos and a couple of huge old jacaranda trees, two luxurious padded recliners had been set out, and he motioned her to one.

They waited in silence while the maid set down a tray of tea things, dainty sandwiches and a coffee gâteau, then he nodded. 'Thank you, Maria. You needn't wait.'

He poured two cups of tea. 'Milk?'

'Yes, please,' Cal said, very formally, and took the pretty, wafer-thin china cup and saucer he held out to her. She ought, she knew, to be keeping up her cool, marginally civil pose—after all, he *had* virtually kidnapped her—but his totally unexpected revelation had only served to increase her lack of composure, and she felt constrained to talk, to cover her nervous embarrassment.

In any case, she was quite incapable of keeping up a hate for more than five minutes, and when a flock of tiny orange butterflies fluttered down on to the statue, sipping moisture from the wet moss, she exclaimed, 'Oh, how pretty! This is a really beautiful garden.'

'I'm glad you like it.'

Luis nodded courteously, like any good host, but she sensed that his mind was far away. He offered her the plate of sandwiches.

'Mmm, cucumber, my favourite—I haven't had

any since I left England.'

'In that case . . .' He put the plate down at her elbow, then sat back, sipping his tea.

She stealthily surveyed him as he stared fixedly across at some point on the far side of the fountain, then, to her horror, found herself saying, 'Your wife——'

His head spun round. 'What about her?'

She crimsoned, but, forced on by something stronger than her apprehension at his forbidding tone, she said lamely, 'Well, I was just wondering what—what happened to her. Was she in a car crash?'

'No.' For a long moment it seemed as though that was all she would get, but then he said slowly, as though to himself, 'Stella was murdered.'

As Cal choked back the gasp of sick horror, he looked at her, bleak-eyed. 'Well, aren't you going to ask me how she died?'

'No!' she blurted out. All her instincts told her something terrible was coming. 'No, I don't want to know.'

But his voice went on remorselessly, as though once he'd begun he could not stop. 'She was American. I met her when I was at law school, and we lived in New York where I was in practice. We were—very happy.'

Cal, overwhelmed by the desolation in his voice, reached out and took his hand, but he gently disengaged it. 'It was in the days of the military junta here. My best friend from school-days, Juan Lopez, was leading the freedom fighters—*Los Hermanos*—he was captured and charged with murder. It was to be a show trial, all legal and correct, but everyone knew the outcome.

'His wife begged me to come back to defend him. I had—a certain reputation for difficult cases, and she thought I might at least show up the sham trial for what it was. So I came. Stella was six months pregnant,' his clipped voice was totally unemotional, 'but she refused to remain behind in New York. We stayed here.'

His eyes wandered across the shuttered windows of the villa. 'On the first morning of the trial, I was on my way to the court-house. Stella had insisted on coming with me. Half a mile down the road, at a junction, a motorcycle drew alongside. I hardly noticed it, then Stella screamed and threw herself across me, just as the pillion rider pulled out a sub-machine gun and began firing. She died in my arms ten minutes later, and I walked away without a scratch. The trial lasted an hour, Juan was sentenced to death, I went back to the States.'

The fountain plashing against the basin . . . birds calling in the trees . . . a silver teapot . . . cucumber sandwiches . . . How horribly, unbearably civilised, against the barbarism of that savage, mindless act of evil.

He was staring down at his cup; she let her glance linger on him, but then looked away, unwilling to be caught prying into his pain.

Of course, it explained everything: his rigid refusal to have dealings with anything political, his implacable hostility to all forms of fanaticism, the lines of strain and grief . . .

She started as she felt a hand rest gently, just for

a moment, on her head, and looked up to see that he was standing, looking down at her.

'Don't be too sad, Cal.' He gave her a faint smile, which brought the hot tears to her eyes. 'It was all a long time ago—more than five years now.'

He moved back from her, and his tone became brisker. 'I've got some business to attend to, but feel free to stay out here. Help yourself to cake, and if you want more cucumber sandwiches, just ring for Maria.' His smile was broader now as he glanced at the empty plate, and Cal blushed as she realised that, without being at all aware of it, she'd eaten the lot, perhaps subconsciously as some sort of antidote against the poison of his story.

He indicated a small silver bell on the tray, and was turning away when he added, apparently as an afterthought, 'Oh, and don't try to leave, of course. There's a security camera on the gate—it's intended to keep out undesirables, but will just as easily achieve the reverse, so . . .' He made an expressive gesture.

'Well, I shall have to leave by eight,' she said very firmly. 'I'm going to a rock concert on the campus.'

'You're not going anywhere—not without me, anyway. And I haven't the slightest intention of going to any rock concert.'

After the traumatic events he'd just been describing, this battle of wills seemed so trivial, so petty, yet here he was, completely back to his old domineering self, and she had to put him right. 'Of course I'm going. There's a group flying down specially from the States. Their last record went to number one, and they're donating part of the proceeds to our——' She stopped abruptly.

'To your . . . ?'

'Our PET fighting fund, if you must know,' she muttered. 'So I must go. My friends will be expecting me—they'll be worried if I don't turn up.'

'Hmm.' He considered for a moment. 'I'll allow you to ring them, later.'

'But what can I tell them?' she called despairingly after him as he turned and headed for the house.

'If you feel that you have to explain yourself, say that you have been unavoidablyd—detained.'

Detained? Well, that was one way of putting it. Cal shot his retreating back a look of impotent loathing, then threw herself back in her chair. She heard his voice from inside the house, then a door closed. She sawed off a hunk of the rich, melting gâteau and took an enormous bite, exactly as though she were snapping someone's head off.

Springing to her feet, she began to prowl around the garden, doing her best to keep out of the line of vision of the house. But a high wall ran all round the grounds, and wherever a tree was growing conveniently close iron spikes had been set in concrete. Perhaps if she carefully balanced the tray, she might just be able to use it as a launching-pad——

'Señorita.'

She jumped and turned to see Señora Valdez just behind her.

'Did you wish something, señorita?' the housekeeper enquired politely.

Instantly, Cal understood the situation perfectly. 'No, thank you,' she said, and, giving the woman a tight-lipped smile, went back to her chair.

CHAPTER NINE

CAL must have remained slumped morosely in the chair without moving for well over an hour. In fact, dusk had fallen and the mosquitoes were starting to whine round her head when Maria appeared to clear away the tea things and she finally roused herself. In the doorway of the house, she almost collided with her host.

'Ah good, I was just coming to fetch you. Your suite's ready.'

She drew a deep breath. 'Will you please get it into your head, once and for all,' she hissed, all too conscious of the maid standing right behind her with the tray, 'I am not spending tonight here. I'm going to ring Ana—she's already asked me to stay with her, after we've been to the concert,' she added meaningfully, 'so I'll ring her now.'

'There's no need. I've saved you the trouble,' he said blandly. 'I've phoned the dreadful Señorita Gutierrez's long-suffering father, and he's letting her know about your change of plan.'

'My——?'

Cal was still weighing up the feasibility of pushing Maria to one side, snatching up an earthenware pot of geraniums standing by the door and smashing it over his head, when he went on, 'Come on—it's time to get changed.'

'What for?'

'You're coming out with me—to dinner.' And he

had put a firm hand under her elbow and was propelling her across the hall, up the elegant, curving marble staircase and along a wide corridor.

He opened a door, flicked the light switch, ushering her past him, and Cal's determination to show no reaction all but evaporated at her very first sight of the room. The predominant colour was peach, so that the whole room glowed softly in the light from two wall lamps: peachy-flowered wallpaper, matching curtains drawn back across white net drapes, a deeper coral-pink carpet and pale wood furniture. Beyond a half-opened door she caught a glimpse of a huge bathroom, with a sunken bath and units of pale marble.

'I hope you'll be quite comfortable.'

Huh, so we were being the perfect host now, were we?

'I imagine so,' she began stiffly, but then, in the face of the charming, ultra-feminine room, the rest of her resolution cracked. She prodded the peach-and-white duvet and rolled her eyes expressively. 'If you knew how rock-hard that camp-bed of Pete's is—I'm surprised I can still walk upright. And as for that bathroom,' she gestured with her head, 'well, I've forgotten what it's like to have a shower that just keeps on coming, let alone a bath——'

'Hmm. It's a relief to find that even you, on occasion, can shed your hair-shirt image,' he replied, quite deadpan, then his eyes flickered over her jeans and pink T-shirt. 'Get changed. I'll be back in half an hour.'

She was about to protest, yet again, that she had no intention of tamely allowing herself to be ordered about by him, but then, instead, gave a resigned shrug. What was the point in arguing the toss with him any longer—it was like beating her head against a quarry-face of adamantine rock—and whatever Ana might secretly think, she at least wouldn't be worried about her, so she might just as well accept the inevitable.

One of the servants must have carried up her rucksack, and Cal unzipped it, pulling out the few clothes she had brought. Well, it would have to be the simple yellow top and vivid yellow-and-white daisy-pattern skirt, which she'd rammed in at the last moment. She showered, promising herself the luxury of a bath the next morning, then shampooed her hair and dried it to a fluffy tawny-gold.

She was just slipping on her white flat sandals when there was a perfunctory knock and Luis came in, attired—surely, that *was* the word?—in a white dinner-jacket and tie, and formal black trousers. She straightened up slowly, her jaw dropping, as he surveyed her critically.

'I'm sorry, but you'll really have to wear something better than that.'

'Too bad—it's all I've got. I'm afraid I seem to have left all my Yves St Laurents back at Chicambo.' She glowered at him across the bed. 'But if you think I'll humiliate you, I could always eat in the restaurant kitchen.'

'OK, OK.' He raised his hands in mock surrender. 'You look charming—no, I mean it,' as she shot him a malevolent look. 'It's just that you seemed to appreciate a few luxuries after Pete's bungalow, so I thought I'd give you a taste of the high life to make up for weeks of Rosa's basic cooking. We've got just about the finest restaurant in Latin America right here in Santa Clara—the only trouble is they're a mite old-fashioned, and wouldn't even let you over the doorstep in that outfit.'

He studied her, his lips pursed. 'Well?' she demanded tartly.

'I was just wondering if I could spruce you up a bit in one of my silk shirts, but no—another time, perhaps. Wait here.'

She heard his quick footsteps recede down the corridor, doors and cupboards banging to—quite close, so his room wasn't far away—and five minutes later he reappeared in black cords and a soft pink casual shirt, his hair still slightly ruffled from the quick-fire change. All at once Cal realised that, just at that moment, more than anything else in the entire world she wanted to reach out and softly smooth that ruffled hair. She ducked to pick up her bag and hide her face, until she felt she could safely meet his eye.

They drove down through the town, along wide, Parisian-style boulevards, through shadowy squares with fountains gleaming in the street lights, couples walking entwined on the paved alleys, then finally along beside the sea. A couple of miles out of town Luis pulled off the road, down a bumpy track to a simple, straw-thatched beach restaurant, with just a long grill barbecue and a few scrubbed tables and chairs set on boards up off the sand. Strings of brightly coloured lights were trailed around the dining area.

'Not quite what I had in mind, but the food's nearly as good here, if slightly less pretentious,' he remarked, as he pulled out a chair for her. 'Now, what will you have? It's mainly fish, but they could probably do you chicken or a steak, if you'd rather.'

She settled on grilled lobster with prawns, served with thick wedges of fresh lime, a huge bowl of tossed salad, and hunks of bread. Washed down with a bottle of flint-dry white wine, it was absolutely delicious, but all the time they were eating Cal sensed the tension, which was always between them whenever they were together, beginning to uncoil unnervingly from the shadowy corners of the restaurant and twine itself round their table, as if isolating them from the other noisy, cheerful diners . . .

'What shall we drink to?' Luis, who had been silent for at least ten minutes, had raised his glass and was looking at her enquiringly. She realised that her eyes, stupidly, were filling with tears and she blinked them away.

'To your work at Palomita—' she spoke with studied casualness '—and to my work—in London.'

He solemnly clinked glasses. 'Very well—to us.'

But that wasn't what she'd said—whatever it was she might have meant. He was twisting her words again.

'London—will you be back there soon?'

'Yes, in a week or so. Pete's coming back then—which will be good news for you, I'm sure.'

He gave her a faintly ironic smile, then nodded

briefly to himself, as though assimilating the information.

She set down her glass and looked away, past him, past the sagging strings of fairy lights, to where the flat disc of silver moon was just sliding up, pointing each wave cap as it rose out of the sea. Down the coast, the lights of Santa Clara twinkled, and behind them the shadowy mountains seemed to float in the blue-black velvet sky.

Without warning, desolation engulfed her. It was all so beautiful, and she was leaving. That slight ache that had twinged miserably like nagging toothache for weeks whenever she'd thought of leaving Chicambo, which she'd so grown to love, was starting up again. To drown it, she took a hurried gulp of wine.

She was setting down the glass when her hand brushed against his. She glanced up and saw that he was watching her intently across the table, frowning to himself. The look held between them for an endless moment, then Cal thought suddenly, What a fool I've been. All this time, and I didn't realise—it isn't just Chicambo, it's *him* that I love!

Her wrist jerked, jarring her glass against his almost full one and spilling most of it.

'Oh, how stupid of me, I'm so sorry.' Her voice shook and she seized her paper napkin, dabbing at his hand, but he snatched it back.

'It's all right . . .' as she began compulsively scrubbing at the table with the ball of damp tissue. 'No—*leave it.*'

His hand closed over hers impatiently, to shake the napkin on to the table, then he dropped it, as though her skin had scalded him, and quickly withdrew his fingers.

She went on looking down at the table, but then realised that the waiter was hovering by them.

'Would you like something else? Ice-cream? Fruit?' Luis's voice was expressionless again, and when she forced herself to look up that horrible cool aloofness was back in his eyes.

She felt the painful humiliation well up inside her. He'd seen that fleeting expression on her face—seen it and understood it; she'd never been any good at hiding her innermost feelings, and he—an intelligent, astute lawyer—could in any case have read with ease that dazed, yearning look. And now, well, he was no doubt cursing himself for ever having got mixed up with her, and working overtime to erect that total exclusion zone around himself once more.

'No, thank you,' she said huskily.

'Coffee?'

'No. I won't sleep if I have coffee now. I-I'm very tired.' She forced a light smile. 'I didn't exactly get much sleep last night, so I'd like to go back now.'

She wasn't really tired—in fact, she was sure that she wouldn't sleep a wink tonight—but at least that should get him nicely off the hook of having to offer to go on to a nightclub, or take a moonlit walk along the beach.

Neither of them spoke a word during the drive back. Cal went on into the villa ahead of him, and had reached her room when he caught up with her.

He took her hand. 'Cal.'

But she pulled it away; she was very afraid that she would break down. 'No—please.'

She fumbled the door open, but he pushed her gently inside and followed her in. He caught hold of her hand again and, lifting it, held it between his, studying the slim, freckled paw, some of the nails broken from scrambling around over fallen trees, several newly healed scratches, then turned it over and softly kissed the palm.

'My dear Cal, I'm so sorry,' he said unsteadily against it, and when she looked up at him she saw that his dark eyes were filled with sadness.

She broke free of him, and thrust her hands behind her back. 'There's no need to be.' Somehow she injected a careless note. 'I quite understand.'

'But you don't—and you must do.' He didn't sound angry, just intensely weary; he sat down heavily on the bed. 'Come here.' And after a moment's hesitation, she obeyed.

'Cal,' he began, then stopped, staring down at the carpet for a long time before giving her a wry, tight smile. 'Ever since I met you I've been torn between the desire to take you apart bodily and the equally violent desire to pull you into my arms and make love to you. Yes,' as she stared at him, her eyes brilliant with shock. He took her hand, and this time she did not snatch it away.

'At Cueltazan, I almost succumbed.' His lips twisted ruefully. 'But I spent most of that night calling myself all kinds of a fool and vowed I wouldn't lay a finger on you again. I've kept very well away from you for weeks, and I was stupid enough to think I'd killed it once and for all, but then, when I saw you again today, well——' he spread his hands in an expressive gesture '—I could have cheerfully murdered you, but at exactly the same time I longed to bring you back here and seduce you. No, not seduce—' he smiled tenderly at her '—for us to make love together.'

The expression in his eyes was a stabbing pain in her insides and she turned her head away, but his voice went on. 'Then, when you looked at me back there, I knew I couldn't do that—take advantage of the tropical night, the moonlight,' his voice was self-mocking now, 'for something that you—we—would regret. For some women, it would be enough, but you, Cal, you must have only the best.'

She swung back to face him again, to gaze wonderingly at him, his face now deeply serious. 'You need—you deserve a man who loves you with all his heart and soul. No reservations, no——' his lips tightened '—no damage. And that I can't provide.' When she continued to look at him, he went on, 'I shall never love anyone again—that's all gone—dead.'

'Yes,' she said slowly. 'I—understand.'

'No, you don't, not really.' He shook his head. 'But I hope that one day you will—that you'll understand, and maybe even be grateful to me.'

He stood up abruptly, then rested his hand very lightly on her head for an instant. 'Goodnight, *querida.*'

Cal stared tensely at the door panel until she heard his door open and close, then mechanically undressed and showered. As she cleaned her teeth,

she gazed at herself, into her deeply shadowed
eyes. He'd been quite right, of course. This time,
at least, he'd been the perfect gentleman. She gave
a shuddering sigh. *But I didn't want him to draw
back. I wanted him to——*

'Stop it!' She spoke the words sharply aloud, as
though her own reflection were arguing with her.
*Haven't you just said that you understand, agreed
that it's better this way—the only way? This way,
you're going home in less than two weeks, with no
bones broken—or rather, no hearts.*

She climbed into bed, switched off the light and
lay for a long time watching the faint pattern of
moonlight across the wall above her head.

The next morning Cal was bathed and dressed by
the time Maria knocked to call her for breakfast.
Luis was already at the table in the beautiful
panelled dining-room. He grunted a civil enough
greeting, but barely looked up from some papers
he was apparently engrossed in.

While they ate, every so often their eyes met, but
then immediately slid away to find something
much more riveting to look at. For Cal, it was an
etching on the wall behind him—by the time
breakfast was over she felt as though she could
have reproduced every pen stroke with her eyes
closed. When their eyes did meet, there was that
altogether new awareness of each other, that silent
agreement that they must keep each other safely
at arm's length.

'Ready?' He was folding papers, ramming them
into a brown manilla envelope.

'Yes.'

'Right, let's go, then.'

Her luggage stood in the hall. He picked it up, together with his own overnight case, too impatient to wait for one of the servants to do it, exchanged a few words with the housekeeper, who was hovering in the doorway, and strode out, leaving Cal just time for a half-smile and a *'Muchas gracias, señora.'*

He was in the driving seat of the Land Rover, the engine already running, and before she could settle herself in her seat he accelerated away, gravel spurting from the wheels, down the drive and out through the gates, which a young man had hurriedly thrown open for them.

As he manoeuvred into the early morning traffic he reached forwards, shuffling through the deck of cassettes, then flipped one out and slotted it in. At once the vehicle was filled with the haunting, sad-sweet music of the country—flutes and plaintive violins—and a tight hand seemed to grip her chest as she thought suddenly, Perhaps this is the last time I shall be alone with him—maybe the very last time I shall see him. And then, feeling tears sting her eyes, she turned away to look out of the side window . . .

Ahead of them were lowering grey clouds, and by the time they reached the mountains it was raining hard, so that Luis was forced to slacken speed, bending forward slightly to peer ahead through the flickering windscreen wipers.

They stopped for coffee at a roadhouse near the summit of the mountain pass, running in out of the rain, and Cal, by dint of not looking at him, managed to keep a trivial conversation going quite satisfactorily, while he toyed abstractedly with the sugar bowl.

They were only about twenty miles from Chicambo when he gave a sharp exclamation and braked violently. Ahead of them, Cal could just see a line of stationary vehicles, and beyond that an enormous slide of yellow mud, like a giant slug, completely blocking the road.

'It's a landslide,' he said unnecessarily. 'They put miles of wire mesh along this part of the road a couple of years back, but still, whenever it rains high up in the mountains, down it comes.'

He got out, slamming the door, and walked off, his shoulders hunched against the rain. He returned a few minutes later, and threw himself in beside her.

'It's a bad one—we'll be here for hours,' he said curtly.

Cal stared at him, her lips tightening miserably. Did he have to make it quite so obvious that he was counting the seconds before he dropped her off?

'But can't we turn back—go another way?'

'Not unless you want a hundred-mile detour . . . Unless——'

He switched on the ignition, reversed until he could turn, then accelerated back the way they had just come.

'I've just remembered—the old road, before they built this one. It runs over the mountains and it'll be rough, but last time I used it it was passable—in this thing, anyway.'

The road was passable—just. Fortunately, the rain had stopped, but for two hours they worked their way up through the jungle, jolting over boulders, edging past fallen tree trunks, lurching along parallel to drops which fell, sickeningly sheer, to the valley floor hundreds of feet below.

Several times, Luis turned to grin at her. His face was flushed, and he was obviously enjoying himself immensely, pitting himself physically against the hair-raising road. 'All right?' he would ask, and she would nod and smile—in spite of the danger, feeling something of his exhilaration grip her.

But then, directly ahead of them, a wide stream cascaded across the road to race away down the mountainside. 'Damn!' He drew up. 'I'd forgotten about this—it's one of the feeder streams to the Rio Clara. It doesn't look too bad, though, in spite of the rain. Hold tight.'

In fact, the water was quite shallow and Cal, peering down, could see it swirling about beneath them. Just as they reached the far bank, though, there was a grinding lurch, and one of the wheels grated against a submerged boulder. The engine whined desperately in the effort to climb out, but the vehicle only bucked impotently backwards and forwards.

They were too heavy. Cal tore off her seat-belt, and even as he shouted 'No!' she jumped out into the knee-high water. She waded to the rear of the Land Rover to find the boulder, pushed hard, and felt it inch forward. Another heave, and it lurched out of their path; the Land Rover's front wheels gripped the bank and it edged slowly out.

Elated, Cal was about to follow when she heard a muffled roar, and, glancing up, she saw a brown, six-foot wall of solid water hurtling down the hillside above her. Oh, God, a flash-flood—and she was standing directly in its path.

Everything, suddenly, was happening in slow motion, like separate frames in a film. Dimly, she heard a door bang open and Luis—his face almost unrecognisable, his mouth open in a shout, his arms held out—was leaping down into the water, but so slowly . . . She took a step towards him, and another, but that terrible roaring was in her ears . . .

He snatched at her, just as the water closed over them both, dragged her to him and swung her round so that he was taking the full savagery of the wave against his back. They were both knocked to their knees like flotsam, the water filling their lungs and clawing horribly at them, so that she was almost torn from his grasp, but then she felt him brace himself against something—a tree root—and begin to haul them both out of the main force of the current.

They lay, wedged against the root, his arm across her, their heads and shoulders out of the water, half stunned and coughing for breath, until, just as suddenly as it had begun, the flood subsided, like a fleeting nightmare, to a far-off murmur and the occasional crack of a branch as it was ripped from a tree trunk.

He climbed painfully to his feet and struggled up the steep, slippery bank, pulling her up after him. For a long time she lay sprawled against him, but at last she drew back and they stared into each other's dirty, hair-streaked faces, as though intent on devouring one another.

'Oh, Cal. Oh, Cal,' he said shakily, and then they were clinging to one another, kissing blindly, burning lips on cold skin. Then—afterwards, she was never sure who made the first move—hands were feverishly tearing aside buttons, zips, seeking the yielding flesh beneath.

Under the arching branches of a roble tree, in a daze of frenzied desire, body leaped to meet body, hands tangled in hair, and each gasped the other's name. In the release of the aftermath of shock which lent a dagger-sharp urgency to their lovemaking, they clutched each other, as though to die in the other's arms, and, like the jaguars on the frieze, each was the hunter, each the prey. Their eyes open wide, as though to drink in the other's ecstasy, the shuddering climax dashed them down, splintering into atoms against each other . . .

Aeons later, Cal slowly opened her eyes. Above her, bees hovered around an orchid on a tree branch, thrusting themselves over and over again at its huge, nectar-laden centre, until, droning drunkenly, they lurched away. She turned her head slightly and saw Luis beside her, lying on his stomach, his head cushioned on one elbow.

His eyes were closed, but he must have felt her faint movement, for he opened them and propped his head on his fist. She gave him a tremulous smile and lifted her hand to caress his face, but he trapped it in his and pressed his lips into the palm before releasing it. He put his hand on her flat stomach, in a gesture of tender possessiveness, then, as he stroked across it and down the curved thigh, his hand froze suddenly.

'Oh, my God.' His horrified eyes flew to her face. 'You were a virgin. I must have hurt you dreadfully. Why didn't you——?' .

But she softly put her fingers across his lips. 'Shh.' She smiled and shook her head, then whispered, 'It's all right—really, it is.'

For a moment, she almost thought she saw tears in his eyes, then he sat up and pulled her up beside him, cradling her to him as though she were made of fragile porcelain.

They stayed there for a long time, quite still, until the sun moved round, burning their arms and legs. Then Luis stood up, lifted her up alongside him, and, reaching for her clothes, which still lay in a damp tangle where they had been fumbled off, he helped her into them before taking up his own.

How beautiful his body was—so strong, and yet so sensitive . . . He caught her eyes on him and smiled, and she smiled back, thinking how, strangely, she felt no shyness, none at all. It was as if, in the violence of that turbulent act of passion, they had passed beyond such emotions as shyness, reserve, constraint . . .

It was late afternoon when they arrived back; the hacienda was lying in a heat-hazed sleep. Luis pulled up on the drive, switched off the engine, then stayed quite still, while she sat quietly beside him.

'Cal,' he said huskily, not looking at her. 'I'd like you, please—to spend the night with me.'

The altogether new uncertainty, the note of

diffidence in his voice, went through her like a sword-thrust. Of course, he was not pretending that anything had really changed. But, whatever might happen in the future, Luis needed her now, and her generous; giving warmth would not allow her to walk away from him—even at the certain cost of pain to her tomorrow, and every other tomorrow. She took his hand and covered it with both of hers.

'Of course I'm staying, Luis.' Then, in an effort to lighten his mood, 'Catch me going back to that horrible spare bed of Pete's before I have to.'

He bent over her hands and softly kissed each wrist, then got out and opened her door. He held her tightly in his arms, then, his arms still round her as though he could not bear to loose her, he led her into the house and up the wide staircase.

CHAPTER TEN

LUIS closed the bedroom door softly and they stood, silent, in the middle of the darkened room, held in each other's arms.

At last, Cal said into his shoulder, 'Luis, can I shower, please, and wash my hair? All that filthy flood water, ugh!' She spoke the last word in a shivering breath, as memory surged terrifyingly back, and he tightened his grip on her.

'Don't think about it. You're here, and I've got you.'

'But—but I haven't thanked you.'

'For what?'

'For saving my life,' she whispered.

He held her even more tightly for a moment. 'My privilege, sweetie. But, if you really want to,' his voice sank to a throaty, intimate murmur which made tingles race up and down her spine, 'you can spend all night thanking me. Just for now, though . . .' He laughed softly. 'As we both stink to high heaven, how about that shower?'

The en-suite bathroom was just as luxurious as the one at the villa—all cream and gold tiles and fittings, the huge bath set in a mirrored alcove, and trailing ferns and vines hanging from a white trellis divide separating the shower area.

Luis made sure there was soap, shampoo, towels, then said briskly, 'Right—I'll leave you to it, then.'

But when she said softly, without quite looking at him, 'You needn't go,' he only smiled at her and began pulling off his mud-streaked shirt.

They stood under the warm jets in the large shower cubicle, their wet, soapy bodies brushing up against each other in a delightful intimacy which Cal had never dreamed of. When she sponged his back she felt tiny ripples of desire run through his hardening body, and sensed the suffocating need spiral inside her in reply—the need that only he had ever awakened, and that only he could assuage.

He swung her up into his arms and lifted her out on to the tiled floor, deliberately letting her flow down his body, then wrapped her in a white bath sheet and set her down at the marble-topped Vanitory unit. He knotted a white towel around his hips, then unhooked the hair-dryer and stood just behind her, his bare thighs touch-caressing her arms and shoulders, drying her hair.

He ran his fingers through it, softly stroking them across her scalp until her hair stood up around her face like a burnished halo and she was swaying slightly on the stool, her eyes narrowed in sensuous pleasure like a sleek little cat under a gently caressing hand.

Raising her to her feet, he held her away from him. 'Has anyone ever told you what a thoroughly sexy face you have? That wickedly full mouth,' he brushed the tip of his little finger across it, 'those golden tiger's eyes,' they flickered beneath the intensity of desire in his, 'and those freckles—yes,' as she pulled a rueful face, 'thoroughly sexy, and

I'm going to kiss every single one of them, before I . . .' he pulled her closer to him, burying his face in her hair '. . . before I . . .' and his voice sank to a low murmur of whispered threats so that she shivered with anticipation.

He released her and gazed down at her with a lop-sided little smile. 'Oh, Cal, what a gorgeous, beautiful, *good* girl you are.'

Wondering at her own wantonness, she gave him a teasing look from under her lashes. 'Just at this moment, I don't feel very good.'

He laughed, rather shakily, 'You know what I mean.'

He returned her look with one composed of such overwhelming tenderness and desire that she thought suddenly, I'd willingly exchange any whole-hearted love that, in the uncertain future, another man might offer me just for the heaven of that one smile from Luis Revilla.

He casually mopped his hair, then lifted her into his arms, carried her back through into the bedroom and laid her down on the wide, cream silk counterpane. He half opened one of the shutters, so that a shaft of light illuminated the beautiful room, furnished in shades of cream and brown, then came and sat beside her.

'Cal,' he took one of her hands and laid it against his cheek, 'there's something I want to tell you. Until this afternoon——' he hesitated '—I hadn't made love to a woman for five years.'

'You mean, since——?' She broke off, and he nodded, his dark eyes on her.

'Yes, since Stella. We were so much in love——'

for a moment, Cal felt a terrible, searing pang of jealousy '—that, after she died, anything less—any cheap, sordid one-night stand, even an affair—well, I just couldn't. So you see,' he flashed her that crooked little half-smile again, 'your macho image of me needs to be rethought somewhat.'

She knelt up beside him, put her arms around him, and laid his head against her breast.

'Listen to me, Luis. I know you don't love me, but I love you.' There, the words were spoken. 'Since that very first day we met, at the airport, I thought I hated you. I told myself I detested, loathed everything about you, but all the time, deep down, I knew the truth and couldn't admit it. But I do love you and I—I want to show you how much. You know now how totally inexperienced I am,' her voice trembled slightly as he put his arms round her, 'so please, teach me—show me how to please you.' As he made no move, she added hesitantly, 'You don't mind me saying that, do you?'

Luis lifted his head and gave her a long look which turned her bones to water. 'Darling, innocent Cal, you offer me the whole of your beautiful self, and ask me if I mind?'

Slowly, he reached forward and unknotted the bath sheet, peeling it back to reveal her small, shapely breasts, then trailed one finger lightly across from centre to centre, so that they rose to meet his barely perceptible touch.

He slid his other arm behind her back and pulled her towards him, bending forward so that his mouth could cup each rosy-brown nipple in turn. His lips, his tongue were toying, circling, his teeth nipping gently, until she felt as though all the sensations in her body were being slowly, inexorably drawn to those two quivering points, and she was suffocating in a rising tide of honey-sweet desire.

She put her hand against his chest, feeling the soft, still-damp whorls of hair, then began stroking the side of her thumb across the flat nipple, until she felt it move and spring to urgent life beneath her touch. She heard him give a faint, throaty gasp, and, pulling him down to lie beside her, let her hands rove down, across his flat, hard stomach towards the tautness of his thighs, but he captured them and held them prisoner.

His eyes were sooty-black, brilliant with desire, and as he held her hands she could feel the tremors run through him, but he said through clenched teeth, as though she was dragging the words from him, 'No—don't, Cal. I don't want to hurry.'

Then, as she gave a murmur of protest, he managed a ragged smile, 'I've got to kiss all those freckles, remember?'

He bent over her and lightly dropped a kiss on the tip of her nose. 'One ...' Another kiss. 'Two ...' Another carefully casual kiss, but his body was shiny with sweat and she could smell the musky scent of his maleness, winding itself around her, and in through every pore in her skin until she was filled with him.

Deliberately, she slid her hand down his side,

over the strong curve of his haunch, paler than the rest of his body, to the pulsating centre of him, throbbing with urgent life.

'Oh, Cal.' With a groan of despairing surrender he rolled over, trapping her beneath him.

At first, neither of them heard the bedside phone, then Luis stilled. He lay for a moment, his heart thumping against her ribs, then, 'Oh, damn—damn—*damn*!'

He slid away from her and snatched up the receiver. 'Revilla here.' It was almost a snarl.

Cal leaned across and gently tweaked the lock of hair which had fallen across his brow. He caught at her fingers with his free hand and began nipping them gently.

'Ramon! Yes, I made an early start this morning. What the hell are you calling for? Don't you know it's five o'clock on a Sunday afternoon? . . . No, I'm not alone.' He flashed Cal a quick grin, and ten seconds later she was blushing scarlet as she translated his Spanish. 'If you must know, I'm in bed with a lovely girl . . . No, you've never met her—and I'll take good care you never do, you old reprobate. Now, what's bugging you?'

Cal hauled herself up and began teasing at the skin on his shoulder, her teeth giving little nuzzling kisses, but then he gave a sharp exclamation, she felt his whole body stiffen, and the next moment he had shrugged himself free from her.

He was listening intently now, then swore with a violence that made her glad that she couldn't understand him, snapped, 'Right, I'll be in touch—and thanks!' and slammed the phone down hard.

He sat with his back to her, his hand still on the receiver, and something about his intense stillness frightened her, although she didn't know why.

'Is—is anything wrong?'

She reached forward and put a tentative hand on his shoulder, but he shook it off with an angry gesture and spun round on her, his eyes blazing with fury.

' "Is anything wrong?" ' he mimicked her voice cruelly. 'You hypocritical little bitch—you know damn well there is!'

He clenched his fists as though he would strike her and she flinched back, but he bunched them together convulsively in his lap.

'Tell me—please.' She looked beseechingly up at him.

'That was a friend of mine, Ramon Juarez—he's a journalist in Santa Clara. He was calling to tip me off—to tell me what you already know.' When she stared at him in utter bewilderment, he went on savagely, 'And don't look at me like that, you scheming. two-faced little cheat, or I'll——'

She scrambled away from him, to huddle on the far side of the bed. All the latent cruelty which she'd seen in his face that first day at the airport was now, for some dreadful reason, being unleashed on her. Her nakedness was making her feel even more vulnerable to his scorching anger, so she snatched up the towel and held it to her. She knew she ought to defend herself, but how could she until she knew what terrible crime it was that she had unwittingly committed?

'But I don't understand——'

'Don't you?' She felt the chill emanating from him, as though a refrigerator door had opened in her face. 'OK, I'll spell it out then. The Home Affairs department's compulsory sequestration of a slice of my land—that's what I'm talking about.'

'*What*? But—but that's got nothing to do with me. I didn't know anything about it, I swear.' Her fingers were picking convulsively at the towel seam, as she sought to still the freezing panic welling up in her.

'No? You and Sanderson—you both tried hard enough to persuade me. *You* got stuck in, that first morning in the forest, or have you forgotten? And when that didn't work, well, the sequestration order was the next move. And don't tell me you've never heard of such a thing—you were all in favour of it to get your hands on that turtle beach. You and that bloody interfering PET group—you've hatched it between you, and your trip this weekend was to celebrate your coup. And what an added spice it must have given to meet up with me——'

'No!' she burst out wildly, then added more quietly. 'You must listen to me. Whatever you think of PET, we just haven't got that kind of influence here, to bring about a government decree.'

'Oh, come off it, honey. You'll be telling me next you don't know that Ana Gutierrez is the favourite niece of the Home Affairs minister.'

Cal was about to open her mouth in vehement

denial when she stopped dead. An ice-cold leaden weight settled where her stomach had been as she remembered, just before the rally on the campus, Ana snatching a fleeting word with her, her brown eyes alight with excited anticipation . . . 'There's nothing official yet, Cal, but I think we'll be giving you an extra-special leaving present to take back to London . . .'

'You can believe me or not, as you choose,' she said simply, 'but no, I didn't know that.' When he said nothing, she ran her tongue round her lips, still trying to grasp fully what he was saying. 'Is—is it just you who's affected?'

He laughed harshly. 'Even I don't merit a whole executive decree to myself. No—all landowners with property over fifty thousand hectares are to have ten per cent compulsorily purchased. And I suppose you approve?'

'Yes, I do,' she said, a spark of defiance igniting. 'I think it's marvellous news. *You* may be trying to work the forest properly——'

'Well, thank you for that unsolicited testimonial,' he broke in sarcastically.

'But there are plenty of others who are abusing their trust. In any case, it's true what I was telling you before. Even you can't hope to manage all your land single-handed—the forest, the plantation, Cueltazan.' She paused, pleading with her eyes for his understanding, but when he did not respond she went on, 'The government can bring in international expertise—maybe they'll even create a national park. It's just a pity that it has to be done this way—by force.'

'It hasn't happened yet,' he said grimly. 'And I'll fight them every step of the way.'

'Yes, you will, won't you?' Anger was stirring in her now. 'That's just what I'd expect from you—fighting for yourself, with no thought of anyone or anything else. *No*,' as his face darkened with anger, 'you've said plenty to me in the last ten minutes—you've presumed to judge me—now you listen to me. You're intelligent, educated—just the sort of person a country like San Cristóbal needs. There's a new, democratic government, struggling to give new hope to all its people. But you—all you can do is squeal when they dare to lay a finger on anything of yours.'

'That's enough——'

'No, it's not.' Some inner conviction that, whatever the consequences, she had to speak—as much for him as for herself—was driving her on. 'If you go on this way, you're going to waste the whole of the rest of your life. Don't think I don't feel for you, Luis—I do, desperately. No one can imagine how you must have felt—the guilt at being spared when your wife was killed.' She saw him wince but, even though it lacerated her tender heart, she made herself continue. 'I can see you ending up like your grandfather, shut away up here, old and embittered, wallowing in self-pity——'

He stood up and swung round to face her. He was breathing so hard that she was sure he was going to strike her this time, but then his mouth twisted and he turned away. He reached into a wardrobe, pulled out a white towelling robe and put it on.

'Wait here. I've got some urgent calls to make—private ones,' he added curtly. 'When I'm through, I'll take you back to Chicambo.'

'You needn't bother. I've walked it before—I can do it again.'

'I said stay here.'

Almost before the door had thudded to with a horrible, dull finality, though, Cal had catapulted to her feet. Her clothes lay together with his on the bathroom floor; her hands were shaking so much that she could hardly pick them up, but somehow she managed to dress herself, all but unaware of the unpleasant drag of the damp garments against her skin.

If only—the thought hammered at her mind—if only the telephone call had come later, then surely Luis would have taken the news differently? Oh, come off it—of course he wouldn't. In fact, the fury at his own weakness would only have served to inflame his anger against her even more.

His words came back to her and she had to clench her teeth against the nausea that clutched at her stomach. His abuse had left her weak; her throat ached with unshed tears, and she longed to huddle down, right where she was, on the tiled floor, and let herself cry as though she would never stop.

But that would be foolish weakness, and she wouldn't give in to it. Her reflection gazed back from the mirror, very pale, the eyes still blank with shock. She stared at herself, frowning slightly as though still in that state of dazed bewilderment, then turned towards the bedroom door.

Noiselessly, she tiptoed down the stairs, carrying her trainers, then in the black-and-white-tiled hall, as she crouched to lace them up, she heard his voice. A door facing her was ajar and, propelled by a need far beyond her fear, she crept across the hall and peeped in. He was sitting at a desk, his back to her, one hand holding the telephone, the other making scrawling patterns with a pen all over a blotter. She couldn't follow the rapid conversation—it was jerky, angry.

I shall never see him again, she thought, and stared at the back of his head for long seconds, that faint frown still between her brows as she struggled to imprint him indelibly in her mind. But it was no use—his image kept shifting and blurring in front of her. She would have to be content, after all, with those few, precious photographs.

The door creaked softly, he half turned, and, terrified, she leaped back, sprinted silently back across the hall and out through the open front door. Her rucksack and bag were still in the back of the Land Rover; she tugged them out and hurried away.

When, thirty seconds later, she risked a glance over her shoulder, she was already screened from the house windows by trees and shrubs. She swung the rucksack on to her back, gripped her bag and set off down the drive, forcing herself to ignore the numbing lassitude that was dragging at her heels. It was a long way to Chicambo and it would be dark quite soon, but she had a lot to do when she got there . . .

She was sitting at the kitchen table, writing, when there was a knock at the outer screen door. For a wild moment she thought, Luis! and her pen skidded violently across the page, but then, hearing a voice, she called, 'Come in—it's not locked, Father.'

'You're up very bright and early, Cal.'

Somehow, she pinned a faint smile into place. 'I could say the same of you, Father.'

'Oh, I was called out to a sick child in the next village. Mercifully, she seems better now.' He looked down at her and Cal's bruised spirit cringed from his penetrating gaze. 'You're very pale, my dear.'

He took a step towards her, and bumped into the travel bag on the floor. His eyes darted round the kitchen, taking in the rucksack, packed to overflowing, her shoulder-bag, the purse and passport lined up beside it.

'Yes, that's right, Father—I'm leaving,' she said brightly, then folded the letter she had been finishing off into an envelope. 'If you could just give this to Pete when he gets back. It's to explain about everything—the plant lists, all the drawings I've made, and so on. Oh——' without looking up, she fished out another envelope and pushed it across the table '—and this is for Rosa. It's all the money I can spare. Tell her——' She stopped to control the tremor in her voice. 'Tell her, I'll miss her very much.'

'Oh, Cal—this isn't the way to go. I—we thought

you weren't leaving till next week.'

She was scrambling her things into her bag in nervous haste. 'Well, I've finished the work I came to do, so I may as well get back.' Her voice was almost casual. 'They're very short-handed in the London office, so they'll be glad to see me, I'm sure.'

At last she looked up at him and, at the gentle concern in his eyes, she was almost undone. But I haven't cried all night, and I won't cry now, she thought fiercely, even though inside she was weeping tears of blood. Pushing back her chair violently, she got up.

'I think I can hear the bus coming up the hill. If I miss it, I shan't get the connecting flight down to Santa Clara.'

She was gathering together her luggage, unzipping her bag to check that her passport, which she had put in ten seconds earlier, was still there, then, finally said, 'Well, goodbye, Father—thank you for everything.'

She held out her hand and saw that, as always, he knew—everything. But he said nothing, just smiled at her rather sadly, and they shook hands.

Just as she bent to pick up her bag, he put his hand gently on her head, '*Vaya usted con Dios*. Go with God, my child.'

CHAPTER ELEVEN

CAL helped herself to another glass of champagne, smiled at the waiter, then retreated to the dimly lit corner she had wedged herself into. Under cover of lifting her glass, she took a surreptitious peep at her watch and stifled a sigh.

Across the room, she heard a familiar laugh and saw Jake, her boss at PET. He was talking to—no, lecturing—some of the minor diplomats' wives, who were designer-outfitted and glossily coiffeured, and he was waving his glass around expansively to emphasise a point. At least he'd had ample time to change into his one and only decent lounge suit—she, on the other hand, had had to come to the reception just as she was, straight from a week in the north of England helping set up an urban wildlife scheme.

She had called off at the PET office, just to tell them she was back, her mind already planning the evening in her flat; pick up a Chinese meal . . . a long, luxurious soak in a hot bath, with some of that new jasmine bath oil . . . chicken and pineapple in her dressing-gown, curled up in front of the fire watching TV . . . perhaps later she would finish wrapping her Christmas presents . . .

But in the office Jake—actually wearing a *tie*, for heaven's sake—had been waiting for her.

'Cal! Where've you been?'

'The train was delayed—points, or something.

Anyway, what's the rush?'

As she picked up the mail from her desk he waved a pair of gilt-embossed cards under her nose.

'We've got an invite to an embassy reception—there's a visiting delegation trying to raise a loan for a new hydro-electric scheme, so there'll be loads of ministers and industrialists for us to buttonhole.'

'Great. When does it start?'

'Half an hour ago,' he said grimly.

'Oh, no! But you needn't have waited—you could have gone without me.'

'I thought you'd want to come—and anyway, it's probably due to you that we've got the invite.'

'How do you mean?'

'It's at the San Cristóbal embassy.' Cal gave a violent start, then somehow covered it by ripping open the envelope she was holding. 'Some of your friends from the PET group in Santa Clara have been pretty active in choosing the best site for the scheme—and maybe it's a thank you for your work out there. You know how much Pete Sanderson's been singing your praises.'

'All right,' she said reluctantly. 'I'll have to change, though.' She indicated her denim skirt, lime-green polo sweater and knee-high boots.

'There isn't time, Cal. And anyway, you look fine, honestly.'

'Well, I suppose they won't expect anything else from PET,' she said doubtfully, then added hastily as he scowled, 'Not that you don't look marvellous, Jake. Just give me ten minutes.'

Once inside the small, dimly lit cloakroom, Cal bolted the door and leaned against it. Would she never get over that awful sick lurch in the pit of her stomach, that tightly clenched feeling in her chest, whenever San Cristóbal was mentioned? But it was getting better—slowly. Just another few months and she should even be able to talk about the place with perfect ease . . .

'Miss Ward, isn't it?'

She turned sharply, to see a middle-aged man at her elbow.

'Yes,' she said warily.

'Oh, forgive me—we didn't meet, of course, while you were out with us. I'm Alfredo Gutierrez, Ana's uncle—for my sins.' He pulled a doleful face and Cal laughed delightedly as they shook hands.

'How is Ana?'

'Thriving—and hatching numerous little schemes, as usual. She'll be so pleased when I tell her I've seen you. I hope you enjoyed your stay in our country?'

'Oh, yes—I really loved San Cristóbal, and the people.' She managed an almost natural smile.

'It's such a pity you weren't able to stay on to see all the changes that are taking place now.' She made a murmur of regret. 'Perhaps you will make a return visit one day?'

'Well, we don't normally do two field trips to the same territory,' she said evasively.

'I see.' He nodded, then glanced around the room. 'I'm afraid some of our people have been delayed—a meeting in the City. But they should be along soon.'

Cal smiled again, but behind her mask of polite interest she was longing to be released from this hot room. Although Señor Gutierrez was far too well-mannered to notice her skirt and sweater, she was growing increasingly conscious of how inappropriately dressed she was. And, besides, three glasses of champagne—or was it four?—on an almost empty stomach were adding a maudlin edge to the mood of depression which she could feel herself sinking into. She realised that he was still speaking.

'The establishment of the national park is a triumph for Dr Sanderson—all his years of effort paying off at last. And, of course, you and your group played their part. It's unfortunate that it had to be by compulsory purchase, but the landowners were given a fair price and they gave in with a good grace—most of them, anyway.'

He grinned at her conspiratorially, then, looking past her shoulder, 'Ah, good, here are the late-comers. Luis!' He raised his voice to call across the room.

There must be a million other Luises in Central America. It couldn't possibly be . . . She willed herself to turn, knowing that she would see a stranger, and—her thought processes all but annihilated—saw *him*, crossing the room towards them.

Dimly, she registered Señor Gutierrez saying, 'You've met Señorita Ward, Luis? She was working near your place in Chicambo.' As Luis inclined his head unsmilingly, he went on, 'Oh, is that the

Environment Minister over there?'

'That's right, Alfredo.' His voice—that voice which she had last heard months before, flaying her soul from her body, so that she had almost physically disintegrated. 'Yes, he's just arrived.'

'Good. I was hoping for a word with him.' He turned to Cal and shook her hand warmly. 'So pleased to have met you, Miss Ward. I shall tell Ana I have seen you.'

'Give her——' she began huskily, aware of the other man beside her, taking in every word '—give her my love, and tell her I think about all of them out there, a very great deal.'

She watched him go, prolonging the moment when she would have to meet Luis's eyes, then finally she steeled herself to face him.

'Señor Revilla.' She half held out her hand, but instead he made a formal little half-bow.

'Señorita Ward.' His voice was cold, slightly detached. 'I hope you are well?'

'Perfectly well, thank you.' You know I'm not, damn you! I look terrible—I don't need to look in the mirror every morning to know that all that vitality, that inner glow I used to have, has faded.

But so had his. She found herself studying his face almost dispassionately—the face she'd seen so often in her dreams. He was thinner, his cheekbones more prominent, his mouth a thin, taut line, his eyes—those marvellous eyes which had, just once, for a few magic hours, looked at her with such——

Oh, God, no! She closed her eyes for a moment against the images—a burning hot tropical afternoon, two figures on a river bank . . . on a cream silk coverlet . . . She took a quick gulp of champagne, jerking the glass to her mouth like a disjointed puppet so that it clattered against her teeth and drops spilled over the brim.

'You're still working for PET?'

'Oh, yes.'

'And you enjoy your work?'

'Very much.' Her enthusiastic tone almost fooled herself. 'I've been spending this week helping on a wildlife project up in Yorkshire.' He nodded, but when he said nothing she went on, 'H-how is Chicambo?'

He shrugged. 'As it was.'

'Is the school open yet?'

'Next year.'

'Father Aidan?'

'He's fine.'

'And Rosa?'

'Well, I believe.'

Could there be anything worse, she asked herself dully, than meeting as a stranger someone who'd once meant the whole world to you? Somehow, she had to break free from this ridiculous, parroting conversation before the superficial veneer cracked beneath her.

'*Señorita*, you do not mind?' She almost beamed at the man who had broken in, putting his hand on Luis's arm. 'Luis, a word?'

They turned away slightly, his sleeve brushing her hand, and she stood, rocking slightly on her feet. On the edge of the conversation, she heard the man say, 'How did the meeting go?' but she didn't catch his reply.

A sob was rising in her, wrenched out of her very vitals, and she began to tremble. Barely conscious of what she was doing, she darted across the room, then in the doorway realised that she was still clutching her glass. She banged it down on a tray, just registered the tinkle of broken glass, then she was running down the carpeted corridor.

The lift was depositing some late guests. She pushed past them, then, as she pressed the ground-floor button, heard someone shout, 'Cal, come back!'

Through the half-open door she saw Luis striding towards her and she gave a gasp of pure terror, shrinking away into the far corner. 'No, I won't.' And then the lift had closed, with a silent purr of satisfaction.

Feverishly, she watched each floor light up in turn, then, as it reached the ground floor, she squeezed out as the doors opened, ran headlong across the foyer and hurled herself out into the cold, evening street.

Her flat was right at the top of an old, four-storeyed house. She slammed the door to, then went across and lit the gas fire; kneeling on the rug, she stared into the flames as she held her icy fingers to the heat, but beyond her pink fingertips her body obstinately refused to warm. She'd probably caught a chill, standing around most of yesterday on that derelict building site or wading up to her ankle-bones in half-frozen mud.

She remembered that in her flying haste she'd

not stopped off at the Chinese take-away. Oh, well, it would just have to be a tin of soup or something—or nothing; as usual, these days, she wasn't really hungry.

In the tiny bathroom, she set the water running, then was suddenly attacked by a volley of violent sneezes. She discarded the idea of luxury bath oil and grimly tipped in half a tin of mustard powder instead . . .

She was just beginning to thaw nicely when dimly, beyond the swirling clouds of steam, she heard someone knocking at the flat door. 'Oh, no. Go away,' she muttered, then relaxed again as the knocking stopped. It had been her landlady—or Mike, the student from the flat below, clutching a pair of socks for her to darn.

But then there was another knock, insistent, peremptory—and this time on the bathroom door.

'M-Mrs Greaves?' she called uncertainly.

'No, it isn't Mrs Greaves.'

Cal turned involuntarily to gape at the closed door, then slid hastily even further down into the water.

'H-how the hell did you get in here?'

There was a soft chuckle. 'Tell me—do you always leave the key in your front door?'

Oh, no! She'd never, ever done that before, but tonight, in her quivering haste to be safely inside, she must have done. But what on earth did he want? Why had he followed her?

'Go away. There's no point in you waiting—I'm in the bath and I'm not coming out.'

'Oh, dear. In that case, I'll have to come in and

fetch you.'

The door-handle began to turn. 'No!' she yelled
in terror. 'Stay there. I'll be out in five minutes.'

When she emerged, reluctantly, in her blue
velour dressing-gown, he was sitting on the sofa,
sprawled back quite at his ease. His black wool
coat was flung casually over the back and the last
flakes of snow were melting in his dark hair. How
handsome he looked—how heartachingly
handsome—but she forced away from her the
treacherous tightness she could feel beginning to
clasp at her chest.

'How did you find out where I live?' she
demanded, looking down at him.

'From your boss—mind you, I had to practically
pick him up and shake it out of him.'

'Well, now that you're here,' she said flatly, 'what
do you want?'

But he didn't answer. 'Have you eaten?'

'No, and I'm not hungry.'

'Well, I am—it's hungry work chasing elusive
females all over London.'

His expression changed and, before she could
leap back, he had straightened up and reached for
her hand. He turned it over, studying it, and she
knew he could see the thinness of the wrist, the
way the bone stuck out, but all he said was, 'You
must be hungry. What can you rustle up?'

'Not much,' she said evasively, then gave a loud
sneeze. 'I was going to pick up a Chinese meal.
There's a good take-away in the next street. If you
want, you could get something from there.'

'And give you the chance to flee the coop, and

catch pneumonia into the bargain? No.' He pulled
her down on to the sofa. 'Sit there. I'll see what I
can conjure up.' He stood up, took off his jacket
and tossed it down on top of his coat. 'Your
kitchen's through there?'

She wanted to tell him to go to hell, but
something peculiar was happening to her vocal
cords, so she merely nodded. Events, as usual
when Luis Revilla was anywhere in the vicinity,
were rapidly moving beyond her control.

She sat listlessly, staring into the fire again and
listening to him moving about in the kitchen, until,
in a surprisingly short time, he reappeared in her
butcher's apron, his sleeves rolled up, and carrying
a tray.

'You like cheese omelette, I hope?'

He set a plate down on her lap, with a feathery
golden omelette, gleaming with melted butter,
which made her mouth water. He went back into
the kitchen and returned with a bowl of lettuce
and tomato salad, and some buttered crackers.

'There didn't seem to be any bread, I'm afraid.'

'No, well, I've been away all week,' she said
defensively.

'Hmm,' was all he said, then sat beside her.
'Now, eat.'

While they ate she tried her best to give all her
attention to the meal, but it was no use; every fibre
of her being quivered with her awareness of his
nearness. She realised he was gazing round the
room, and when he caught her eye he said, 'Don't
mind me. I'm just curious to see the place where
you live.' He shot her a sideways look. 'No snakes

in plastic bags here?'

He grinned at her disarmingly and she almost smiled back, but then dropped her eyes to her plate, telling herself, *No*—remember that last afternoon.

When they had finished, she got to her feet. 'I'll make some coffee.'

In the kitchen, she leaned up against the unit waiting for the coffee to percolate. Oh, why had he come? And why wouldn't he go? Was he so insensitive? Surely, he must realise, after her tremulous confession of how she felt for him, that his coming here could only bring her fresh pain?

Back in the sitting-room he was flicking through a ringed folder of colour photographs that he must have taken up from the side table. Oh, no—next year's PET calendar, waiting to replace this year's on her kitchen wall. She stood watching, waiting for the inevitable moment, then his hands suddenly stilled.

'It-it's come out quite well, hasn't it?' she said as she made herself look down at the huge white angel's trumpet flowers, just opening against a brilliant blue sky.

Her hand shaking slightly, she went to pour his coffee.

'No, not yet, Cal. I want to talk to you.' He caught her hand and drew her down beside him again, then gently turned her face to his. His lips tightened. 'I suppose I don't deserve any better than that you should look at me like some wild creature that isn't at all sure what it's going to do next.' He looked at her, a deep seriousness now in his eyes. 'That dreadful afternoon—can you forgive me for all the vicious things I said to you?'

'Of course—it doesn't matter,' she said woodenly.

'Yes, it does.' There was anger in his voice now—anger at himself. 'I behaved abominably, and the worst thing is I knew all along, somehow, that you were innocent, that you knew nothing about the land. I was terrified at what you were making me feel, you see, and so I jumped at the chance to shake myself free of you once and for all—whatever the cost to you.'

At the ravaged look on his face, the chill inhibition which had held her still began to melt, and she put her other hand on his.

'I actually thought I could do that, you see,' he said wryly. 'I forced myself not to chase after you, and when I found you'd left Chicambo I told myself it was all to the good. The only trouble was, once you'd gone I couldn't get out of my mind what you'd said to me.'

Her hands tightened on his, but he smiled at her. 'I began, slowly, to see that you'd been right. I just couldn't go on cutting myself off from life forever.'

He paused again, then, 'Aren't you in the least curious as to why I'm in London? No?' when she did not answer. 'I'm on this delegation as a member of the government—I'm in the justice department, helping to draft a new constitution, but I managed to persuade them that they needed a good lawyer on this trip.'

'Oh, Luis, I'm so glad,' she said simply. 'But what

about the estate?'

'Well, I'm finding I can't give so much time to Palomita and the forest—maybe it's as well I'll soon be losing thirty thousand hectares of it.'

'Is-is that how much they're buying off you?' she asked hesitantly.

'Not buying—no.' He gave her a long look. 'I'm offering that amount free and in perpetuity to form the national park of Chicambo. That's if——' He stopped.

'If?'

'If I can borrow a PET on long-term loan to help set it up.' Then, when she could only stare at him, he said huskily, 'Oh, Cal, for God's sake, come back with me.'

Come back—to Chicambo? As national park warden? Her heart leapt for an instant, then fell again. Seeing him, consulting him, working with him? No, she couldn't possibly.

He was going on, rapidly. 'I should have been warned, the first time I set eyes on you. Heaven knows I've cursed myself often enough for not leaving you on that bench at the airport. But you'd elbowed your way into my life—you were like one of those damned chiggers. I tried to shake you off, but you'd burrowed deep into my hide, and the more I scratched at the wound, the worse it got.'

Gently, he took both her hands in his and held them. 'That cursed afternoon when you told me you loved me,' his voice was ragged, 'you offered me a gift that I was too blind, too bigoted to appreciate—yourself. Warm, life-loving, life-giving.'

At the expression in those sooty eyes, peculiar

feelings of elation were fluttering dizzily around inside her. 'My darling, beloved Cal, before I go quite crazy—marry me.'

'Oh, yes, Luis.' And at last she went into his arms . . .

A long time later, he murmured against her hair, 'My darling, do you think your parents would object to a Christmas wedding?'

'Mmm, snow and the village church,' Cal said dreamily. 'And then we'll ask Father Aidan to bless the marriage in Chicambo.'

'He'll be delighted, I've no doubt,' he said drily. 'He's been pointing out at weekly intervals, for months, that at my age it was high time I remarried and had a family.' He gave her a tender, meaningful glance, which made her blush peony-pink with confusion. 'Then, the morning I left for London, he asked me, very casually, if I *should* happen to see you, to give you his best wishes.'

Cal was beginning to feel light-headed with happiness. Just a few hours before, she'd walked into the PET office carrying that invisible lump of ice that went everywhere with her, and now . . .

'I must ring Mum and Dad.'

He shook his head. 'No, I think we should tell them in person. After all, they ought to have the chance to give their prospective son-in-law the once-over.'

'Well, I was going down tomorrow, but with this cold I'd decided to spend the weekend in bed—I mean——' She broke off as Luis gave her a slow, wicked smile.

'A much better idea. Did I ever tell you I've got a sure-fire remedy for colds? No? Well, I'll tell you about it, later. But first—I never did finish kissing all those delicious freckles, did I?'

He put his thumb beneath her chin, gently tilting her face to his, and his lips gently brushed against her cheek.

'One . . .' Another kiss. 'Two . . . three . . .' Then he raised his head. 'You know, *querida*, I have a feeling that this is going to take all night.'

'Oh, I don't mind. As long as it's all part of your sure-fire cure, that is—take as long as you like.'

Cal gave him a deliberately seductive glance from under her lashes—then completely ruined the effect with a loud sneeze.

Back by Popular Demand

Janet Dailey
Americana

A romantic tour of America through fifty favorite Harlequin Presents® novels, each set in a different state researched by Janet and her husband, Bill. A journey of a lifetime in one cherished collection.

In June, don't miss the sultry states featured in:

Title # 9 - **FLORIDA**
　　　　Southern Nights
　　#10 - **GEORGIA**
　　　　Night of the Cotillion

Available wherever
Harlequin books are sold.